PIT & MISS MURDER

A BARKSIDE OF THE MOON COZY MYSTERY
BOOK FOUR

RENEE GEORGE

BARKSIDE OF THE MOON PRESS

Pit and Miss Murder

(Barkside of the Moon Mysteries Book 4)

Copyright © Renee George 2019 – All Rights Reserved

Print ISBN: 978-1-947177-30-7

When Lily Mason's uncle is accused of murdering a prominent Moonrise citizen, the amateur detective and her loyal pit bull Smooshie must dig out the truth and find the real killer.

Integrating isn't easy for a shifter in an all-human town, but Lily Mason is finally making it work. She has love in her life, enjoys a great job, attends community college, and best of all, her fixer-upper house is nearly livable. She couldn't be happier.

Until her Uncle Buzz is accused of murder.

A prominent member of the community has been found murdered in the parking lot of her uncle's cafe, The Cat's Meow. And thanks to a contentious relationship with the victim, Uncle Buzz is the number one suspect.

Now Lily, Smooshie, and the Moonrise gang must solve the murder before Lily's only family ends up behind bars.

For all the fur babies still waiting for forever homes.

CHAPTER 1

"What do you think, Lily? Veil or no veil?" Theresa Simmons sat at the office desk in front of the computer and pointed at a sleeveless wedding gown on a bridal website.

I filed April's expense sheets and closed the cabinet. Thanks to a large donation of four-thousand dollars the month before, along with our regular donors, the rescue had managed to have a little extra left over to put finishing touches on the new shelter Parker Knowles, the owner of the Moonrise Pit Bull Rescue, had started building two years ago. Between fundraisers, volunteer efforts, and some directed donations, Parker's vision to save as many of these beautiful animals from awful circumstances looked to be a reality.

We finally had our new permits in order, and next week, we planned to move our current nine rescues over to the new place after Parker and a whole team of helpers finished the fencing for the outdoor play spaces this weekend. I was most excited that we'd have room to take in another fifteen furbabies until we could find fosters or forever homes for them. I hoped our open house, not this coming Saturday but the next, would raise a lot of money and get more people interested in volunteering or fostering.

Watching the transformations of the rescues was like living a lifetime in a few months as they went from injured, damaged, starved, and sometimes very ill dogs into energetic, loving, trusting, and healthy babies ready for forever homes. Not all of them turned around so fast, but even furkids who had trouble finding a way to trust, like our shelter mascot Star, who had been with us for over a year and a half now, deserved to be treated with love and kindness, whether they were ultimately adoptable or not. Parker and our team of pit bull lovers were virtual magicians, and their devotion to rescue gave me hope every day.

Last night, he'd taken in a year-old pup whose inflamed skin hung loose with severe mange that had taken most of his hair. So other than a black nose, we weren't sure of his coloring. The poor boy had trembled, his tail tucked and his head down. Parker stayed with him until early this morning. I'd been with Parker for Sunday Night Spaghetti, a weekly thing for us, when the call came in. I helped him with the paperwork and getting the isolation room ready. After, I'd stayed the night at Parker's house (for the fourth night in a row), and when I got up, I went over to take the morning shift so he could get some sleep.

Parker had been cuddling the sick dog and whispering words of encouragement. The pup's tail wagged when Parker had told him what a good boy he was, which had been a big improvement from the night before.

If I hadn't been in love with Parker already, that scene would have sent me all the way into my feelings. As it was, my heart had felt full to bursting. We'd been an official couple for almost a year, and our dating anniversary was fast approaching. He knew who and what I was, a cougar-shifter with a traumatic past, and it hadn't scared him off. Well, not after he'd had a minute to process, and by a minute, I mean the longest four months of my life. But here we were, going on a year, and I'd never been so happy. Frankly, it scared the heck out of me.

The dogs in the shelter, as if reminding me of how happy they were to be here, too, suddenly began barking with excitement.

I peered at the clock. It was noon. Lunchtime. Which meant Keith Porter, one of those awesome volunteers and Theresa's boyfriend, had probably just taken kibble back to them.

"Lily? Did you hear me?" Theresa asked, snapping her fingers to get my attention. "Veil or no veil?"

I rolled my eyes. "I think you should get a divorce before you start planning your next wedding."

"Spoilsport," she said. Her lower lip jutted into a pout. "Why won't you let me dream?"

"I'm happy to let you dream." I grabbed my purse. "I'm off to dream myself."

"That's right. You start summer classes today." Her expression soured. "I'm not sure how I feel about you getting all educated," she teased. "Next thing you know, you'll be too good for the likes of us."

"I'm too good for you now," I replied. This was my fourth semester doing general studies at Two Hills Community College. If all went well this summer, I could start the Veterinarian Technician program in the fall.

"Well," Theresa said on a laugh, "then we're really in trouble!"

I giggled. "I'm not going anywhere anytime soon." As long as Parker wanted me around, there was zero chance I'd leave. Besides, I hoped my education could be a resource for the shelter. After all, I would be qualified, as long as I worked under the supervision of a vet, to provide care for the dogs we took in. I gazed at Theresa. "You know, it's going to take at least another year before I get my associates degree, and another two if I want to be a technologist."

"If?"

"Technicians can do just about everything a technologist can, and I can start practicing sooner." I shook my head. "Either way, I don't plan on giving up my duties here at the shelter." Although, juggling full-time classes, my shifts at the shelter, and Petry's Pet Clinic had been a time-management nightmare. I worried sometimes that my relationship with Parker would suffer, but he had been nothing but encouraging and supportive.

Theresa stood up and embraced me. "I'm glad." Her voice choked with emotion. "I don't know what we did before you got here."

"Are you okay?"

Theresa wiped at her eyes. "I'm fine. Just happy."

I narrowed my gaze at her. Emotional, talking about marriage, demonstrative, and she'd been using the bathroom more frequently. "Are you pregnant?"

"How in the world do you always do that?"

"So, you are?"

"Yes." She hugged me again. "Keith is so excited, but we have to keep it under wraps until the divorce is final. Three more weeks! I can't wait to get that bastard out of my life for good."

"I'm happy for you," I told her, and I was. But I was also worried. Jock Simmons was a Grade-A jerk and a wife beater, but he was also a smart-as-a-whip lawyer. He was still on the town council, even after he'd been turned into a pariah when he'd smacked Lacy Evans at the hospital a little over a year ago, and he'd been arrested for assault. That took an incredible amount of pull. It was the first time Theresa's dad, Sheriff Avery, had seen Jock as an abuser. When the sheriff had confronted Theresa about it, she'd told her dad everything. It had given her the courage she needed to finally leave Jock.

Unfortunately, Jock had managed to get the charges knocked down to a misdemeanor and had only had to pay a fine. Rotten bastard. Jock's standing as a council member and as a family lawyer to over half of Moonrise, along with Lacy's reputation, had made it hard to get a felony conviction. And, since Jock was a top-notch in his field, he knew all the tricks to make Theresa's divorcing him next to impossible.

I worried this pregnancy would give him the ammunition he needed to make sure she ended up with nothing but the clothes on her back.

Still, I'd rather be naked than married to Jock Simmons, so Theresa would still be better off than before she'd left him.

"You and Keith will make amazing parents," I told Theresa, because regardless of the battle to come, I believed they could weather it.

She smiled. "Thanks, Lily." Her smiled turned into a frown. "You won't say anything, will you?"

"Cross my heart," I said.

Jordan Deeter, a college student majoring in graphic art and one of our newest volunteers, knocked outside of the office door. Her blonde hair was pulled back into a pony-tail. She wore jeans, a pink T-shirt that said Show Me Your Pitties, and a pair of hot pink, chunky-soled, lace-up tennis shoes that gave her a slight height advantage over me.

In other words, she was a shorty like myself, only where I was built like a stick, Jordan had curves for days. I envied her as much as I liked her. Recently, though, I think she'd started using vinegar as a hair rinse, or maybe for feminine hygiene. Either way, I'd never been keen on the scent, so it rankled my nose. Still, I wasn't going to be rude about it.

"Hey, girls," she said. She held out a handful of mail. "This was in the mailbox. I hope you don't mind that I brought them in."

I took the small stack of mail from her and shuffled through it. Electric, phone, junk, junk, and an envelope marked *City of Moonrise, Department of Permits, Licensing and Inspections*, and it had the words, *Important: Needs Immediate Response*, stamped across the front.

"Thanks," I told her.

"Is everything okay?" Theresa asked.

"Sure," I said. At least I hoped so. The inspection for the new facility was a week away, so I couldn't understand why we were getting notified, or what it could be about. I opened the letter, the paper hissing as I pulled it apart.

Inside was a notice from the City of Moonrise that the rescue, the current shelter, was being cited for zoning violations regarding overgrowth of flora near the fence, spalling, and chipped paint. And it gave an appeal date but warned that we could be fined up to two hundred dollars a day in fines from date of issue until these issues were fixed. On top of that, if we appealed, there was a chance the fines could go up to a thousand dollars or more.

I groaned when I saw the date of issue. It was five days ago. It was signed by E. Laverty, Zoning Compliance Officer.

I swear if I'd been a teapot, steam would have whistled from my ears. "Son of a garbage eater."

Jordan joined us at the desk. "What's wrong?"

I slammed the letter down. "We're being cited for nuisance violations."

"Why?" Jordan asked.

"I have no idea. We passed our licensing inspection two months ago, but according to this, we have weeds along our fence and chipping paint." I pointed to one word I wasn't sure of. "And spalling? What in the actual heck is spalling?"

"Broken concrete," Theresa said. "Usually a sidewalk." She appeared a little gray as the color left her cheeks. "Oh, gosh, Lily. I think this is my fault."

I stared at her. "How in the world is this your fault?"

"Clem Hanley is the chair of the zoning commission. He and Jock are old law school buddies. This could be retaliation."

"But why would he come after the rescue?" Jordan asked. She might have been new here, but Theresa's separation was town talk. When both Theresa and I turned our gazes on her, she blinked sheepishly. "I'll go see if Keith needs any help."

After she left, I turned my attention back to Theresa. "Do you really think Jock would come after the shelter?"

Her green eyes brimmed with tears as she nodded. "He threatened to ruin everything I loved. This place is at the top of the list for me. Besides," she sniffed, "he hates you, Lily. For some reason, he counts you as one of the reasons I left him."

"And why would he do that?"

She shrugged. "Because you are. Before I met you, I'm not sure I would have had the strength to do it. The idea of upending my life and starting over petrified me. But you did it, and you're so happy now. It made me believe I could do the same." Her voice caught, and she took a deep breath before continuing, "I told him as much the night I left, when he said I would never make it without him. He'd gotten so angry when I mentioned you." She sat down in a nearby chair, her shoulders slumping as she stared at the floor. "I'm so sorry, Lily. I'm sorry my messy life is spilling over onto the rescue.

I went to her and squeezed her shoulder. "We don't know for sure this is Jock's doing." There was a small faction in Moonrise who was not crazy about having pit bulls in town. Any one of those jerks could have called in a complaint. Besides, even if it was Jock, Theresa wasn't responsible for his bad behavior, and it wouldn't change our circumstances to blame her. "Why don't you call the number on the notice and find out what's going on, and I'll go wake up Parker."

CHAPTER 2

The frantic patter of claws hitting the hardwood floor made me grin as I waited for my big girl to barrel out of the hallway and into the living room to greet me. She went up on her back feet, her butt wiggling so much she missed me with her front paws.

"Hey, Smooshie-girl." I laughed, wrapping my arms around her waist when she was back on all fours and giggling more when her tail swished against my hair. Her volleyball-sized head pressed against my hip, her rusty-brown and white body vibrating with excitement as I scratched her butt.

"What are you doing awake?" Usually, when she tucked in during the day, she was down for the count.

She panted, turning in a circle and giving me a high-pitched yip.

"Is that so," I said in response.

A deep, masculine voice startled me. "Do you speak dog now? Because that skill could come in mighty handy."

I glanced up from Smooshie to see Parker standing in the kitchen doorway, his dog Elvis, a silver-blue pit bull-Great Dane mix, next to him. He stared at me. His blue eyes intense, but with a half-teasing smile tugging at his lips. He wore flannel pajama bottoms and nothing else. His broad chest made my mouth water, and I swallowed fast to keep from drooling.

"Why aren't you still in bed?" I asked. He'd been exhausted when he'd left the rescue this morning, and I had expected to have to wake him up. He looked so good, happy, right now. I hated to spoil it with bad news.

"I think Smooshie must have eaten something that didn't agree with her. She's had a couple bouts of the runs today."

Smooshie's wide face split into a huge grin, her tongue lolling out the side as if to say poop happens. I knelt beside her, unable to hold her still long enough for a good examination of her gums, nose, and eyes. "Do you think she's sick?"

"She's drinking water, and, as you can see, she has lots of energy, so most likely she'll be fine when whatever upset her gut passes. Did she eat anything weird last night?"

I flushed guiltily. "Maybe." I'd taken her with me to the Cat's Meow Diner the day before for lunch, and I'd caught her begging for food at one of the tables. "Do you think it could be onion?" I'd learned that onions, even cooked ones, could be toxic to dogs. I pulled my phone from my purse. "Should we call Ryan?" Ryan Petry, the local veterinarian, was a good friend to Parker and myself. Right now, I was grateful to have him on speed dial.

Parker crossed the room to me and stroked his fingers down my arm. "Her diarrhea wasn't bloody. That's a good sign. Other than the squirts, she seems to be doing okay. I'll keep an eye on her while you're at class. Trust me, if I think she's in danger, I'll drive her over to Ryan's clinic immediately."

Class. Between the notice and Smooshie's tummy upset, I'd almost forgot about school. "I think I better skip today."

"Nope," Parker said. "I promise to call if Smoosh worsens."

"It's not that," I told him. I peered down and fidgeted with the hem of my shirt for a second. "You're needed at the shelter. A letter from the city came this afternoon. It says you have some zoning violations, and you'll be fined for every day they aren't addressed." I hastily added, "Theresa is calling the zoning office to find out what we can do."

Parker frowned. "This happened once before, and unfortunately, it's not something that we can take care of in an afternoon. But I'll get it sorted. I don't want you to worry about it." He dipped his head and placed a gentle kiss on my lips, then smiled. "Now, you don't want to miss your first day of summer classes."

His relaxed manner eased my own tension. I smiled back and let my gaze travel from his face to his naked chest. I wiggled my brows. "Maybe I do."

He encircled my waist with his arms and pulled me in close. "Ditching school. Such a bad girl."

I giggled for a second—then gagged as an overwhelming stench, of what could only be described as raw sewage and spoiled eggs, wafted and clung to the air around me. "Oh, Goddess. Smooshie," I said, my tone two octaves lower than normal. I gazed down at my gorgeous pittie as she danced around our legs, her tail whacking me in the calves. I pushed away from Parker and cast him a piteous look as I waved my hand back and forth in front of my nose. "Girl, there was nothing ladylike about that stink bomb."

Parker wrinkled his nose, and Elvis whined. "I think someone needs to go outside again."

The smell had texture to it, and my werecougar senses were entirely overwhelmed. Not even Parker's aroma of honey and mint could cover up the *Eau de Poopoo* Smooshie was serving. "I think that's the universe telling me to go to class."

"Smooshie is a garbage eater, so her eating several universes would not surprise me one bit," Parker said.

The odor doubled in potency. Goddess in a green tutu, the

methane leaking from the loveable pit bull's butt could accelerate global warming to crisis levels.

Parker's lip curled as he gave Smooshie an incredulous stare. He turned his gaze back to me. "She'll be fine. Promise." His nasal tone told me he was avoiding breathing through his nose.

I didn't blame him. I'd stopped breathing through my nose the moment the smell hit. Still, I swear it was seeping in. "If you're sure…" I was already walking backward toward the door.

He shooed me. "Go on. I'll see you after class."

"I'll see you in a few hours. Or sooner if she gets worse or you need me."

"You got it." He winked and gave me a cute finger wave then scratched Smooshie's ear. Then he waved his hand across his face dramatically. "Oh," he said, shaking his head and taking Smooshie's collar. "Come on, girl. Out with the bad."

I cast him a grateful smile before closing the door between the biohazard and myself.

THE FIRST DAY OF THE SUMMER SEMESTER AT TWO HILLS Community College teemed with life. College students young and old walked the paths between buildings carrying heavy backpacks and satchels on their way to becoming their dreams.

Or at least that's how it always felt for me.

My one-thirty-in-the-afternoon, once-a-week-on-Mondays, three-hour chemistry class—two hours of lecture time with one hour of lab—had lasted exactly twenty-three minutes. Enough time for the professor, Dr. Marigold Robbins, an older woman with long gray hair that flowed over her shoulders like a lion's mane, and who carried off bohemian chic with flair, to go over the syllabus and warn us that missing even a single class could lower our grade. I overheard three young men whispering about dropping the class. Dr. Robbins—whose hearing, it appeared, had not diminished with age—encouraged them to go with their gut.

I knew from some of my fellow students that there were many of them, too many, who were only going to school because it's what their parents wanted. I had wanted to go to college for so long that their ambivalence toward education made me sad.

My other two summer courses were on the Tuesday-Thursday schedule. The first one at eight in the morning and the second one at nine-thirty. I'd just did a search for the classrooms and was on my way back toward the parking lot. I wanted to get back to Parker's and check on Smooshie. Parker and I weren't living together, but I did spend a lot of time there. The renovations on my old house were coming along slowly. And with school and fewer work hours, I didn't have time or money to finish anytime soon.

Parker didn't seem to mind one bit. He'd hinted several times about me moving in with him, but I wasn't ready to give up on my own place. I'd never owned anything other than my truck, and too many times I'd been the victim of other people's greed and cruelty. There was something about having a house and property in my name that was completely paid off that made me feel secure. Even if the house wasn't livable, and I had to stay in a small used trailer for the time being.

I took a deep breath, inhaling the scents of spring, as I crossed in front of Davis Auditorium toward the front lot. Spring had arrived late this year after a particularly long, cold winter, so the redbuds, magnolia trees, lilac bushes, and dogwoods were just now in bloom, creating a perfumed array of purple, pink, and white landscape. The sidewalks were heavily dusted with yellow pollen, the layer thick enough that you could see shoe print moving in all directions. A sneeze from a student in desperate need of allergy medicine drew my attention.

I recognized the guy. James Hanley. He walked with purpose, his shoulders rounded and his head down, going in my direction, only at a much faster pace. He'd been a high school buddy of Addy Newton, a good kid and one of our past volunteers.

James, as I recall, was a troubled youth and a bit of a real jerk. He'd been part of the group who had urged Addy to shoot his .22 rifle off in town and nearly put a hole in me.

I'd ducked in time, and he hit my truck door instead, thank heavens.

I'd learned to really like Addy. He'd turned his life around and had become another member of my extended Moonrise family, but his friend James was another story.

I stepped to the side when he got close to me, but still, he nearly clipped me with his elbow. "Hey," I said, feeling surly.

James muttered, "Watch where you're going," and kept walking toward the mostly full parking lot.

Ugh. I shook my head. Getting out of high school had done nothing to grow him up. He was still a jerk.

I was still watching him speed walk ahead of me when a chorus of, "Look out!" "Heads up!" and similar shouts put me on alert. I glanced up to see a small round object the size of a baseball winging toward my head. Thanks to my supernatural reaction time, I reached up and snatched it from the air before it could nail me.

I examined the object. It was not only the size of a baseball, but it was also, in fact, a baseball.

A young man about two hundred feet away, near the auditorium, trotted toward me. I could hear him cussing and thanking God he hadn't hit me. I smiled.

"Stay there," I said, waving him back. He slowed to a halt.

I'd played catcher on my high school softball team, and I used to have a deadly arm, but it had been two decades since I'd thrown a ball. I reared back and let go, delighted when the young man caught the ball.

He waved his gloved hand at me and shouted, "Thanks, Miss!"

"No problem," I yelled back.

"That's some arm you got there, Lily," a familiar voice said.

I smiled as my friend Ryan Petry caught up to me. "What are you doing here?" I asked. "I thought you weren't teaching any classes during the summer."

Ryan taught a few courses at Two Hills for the vet tech program during the fall and spring. His perfectly coiffed hair ruffled in the breeze, and he ran a hand through it to smooth it down. "I had to attend a mandatory adjunct meeting today." He shook his head. "I like teaching. It's everything else that goes with it that makes me think about quitting every year."

"Well, you can't quit until after I'm done. I need all the allies I can get."

"From what I hear, you're a bit of a teacher's dream."

I flushed with pleasure. "I really love learning. If there was any money in it, I'd become a professional student."

Ryan laughed, and it was a sound that could break a thousand girls' hearts if Ryan happened to be interested in girls. But he wasn't. Ryan Petry, the local heartthrob, was gay, a fact not many people knew. Small southern towns weren't known for having liberal values, but I'd grown up in a shifter-witch community, and I knew that who a person was attracted to and who they loved was ingrained in their DNA. Still, I would keep Ryan's secret as long as he wanted it to remain so.

He put his arm around my shoulders. "Can I walk you to your truck?"

"Yes, sir," I said. "If I can get some advice from you on the way."

"Sounds like a fair trade," he replied. "Is this about school, romance, or a certain wrecking ball named Smooshie."

I giggled. "It's Smooshie. She had some diarrhea this morning, and I'm worried she might have gotten into something at Buzz's diner yesterday afternoon. Parker says she'll be all right, she's active, drinking water and eating food, but I don't like to take chances with her."

"Parker is one of the most in tune people I know when it comes to dogs, especially pit bulls. If he's not worried, I think Smooshie is going to be a-okay. He's right. If she's active, and drinking and eating like she normally does, chances are once she's pooped out whatever has irritated her belly, she'll be fine. If you are really concerned, though, bring me a stool sample, and I'll get it analyzed for you."

"Thanks, Ryan." I leaned into him and gave him a friendly nudge. "Hey, we got a notice today that the rescue was being cited for zoning code violations. Parker says this has happened before, but not since I've been in town. The daily fines seem pretty steep."

Ryan's brows furrowed. "I got a notice three weeks ago. It was for a slight crack in the concrete on the sidewalk leading into the clinic. The damage probably happened because of the cold winter contracting the concrete and the suddenly warm spring, causing it to swiftly expand."

"What did you do?"

"I sealed the crack and paid the fine. It cost me eight hundred dollars." He shook his head. "Talk about highway robbery. If I hadn't heard about Albert Langdon having to pay double the fines at his appeal, I might have tried to fight it, but it just wasn't worth the risk."

"How would the city even know you had a cracked sidewalk?" I asked.

Ryan shrugged. "Someone complained. Maybe a customer. Maybe a neighbor. Though I can't think of anyone malicious enough."

Theresa had said Jock was angry with me. Could he be taking his anger out on the people I care about? Ryan? Parker? Who's next? Buzz, Nadine, and CeCe all came to mind. "I'm sorry, Ryan."

"It's not your fault, Lils." He unlooped his arm from my shoulder as we approached the driver side of my small, green rust-bucket of a truck. "Unless you're the one who called in the complaint."

"I'm not," I assured him. "Thanks for the walk and the talk. I'll get a fecal sample over to the clinic this afternoon."

He gave me a two-finger salute. "I'll be there."

As I got into the truck, I couldn't stop the coiling tension winding in my gut. Two notices could be a coincidence, I told myself, but I knew no amount of rationalizing would satisfy me until I checked on Buzz.

CHAPTER 3

I t was after two in the afternoon by the time I got to The Cat's Meow. The diner was empty with the exception of Opal Dixon and her sister Pearl. The two elderly ladies sat at their favorite booth, the one in the back corner where they could watch the other tables while also keeping an eye on the goings-on in the parking lot.

Opal, with her cotton ball hair, was the more serious of the two, and I'd found out the year before that she would and had done almost anything to keep her sister safe from an abusive husband who'd had ties with the mob in Vegas. Pearl, the quirkier, had her hair dyed hot pink today, and I applauded her bold choice of color.

When I'd first arrived, I'd been targeted by a poison pen threatening to spill my secrets. I'd worried that my werecougar status was about to be exposed, but it turned out it had been Pearl amusing herself by baiting people in town and seeing if any of her guesses might land on the truth.

Since I'd found her out, Opal had promised to end Pearl's poison pen days.

"Lily!" Pearl said brightly. "Come join us."

"I'm sorry," I told them. "I can't right now. I have to talk to Buzz." I looked around the diner. "Where's Freda?" Freda was Buzz's waitress, and she was always here during the day.

Opal shrugged. "Buzz is pulling double duty."

Pearl cackled. "It's okay, though, we just keep getting our coffees refilled so we can watch him come and go."

"Pearl!" Opal said, but her smile told me that Pearl wasn't wrong.

"You know I don't mind taking care of my two very best customers," Buzz said as he walked out of the kitchen and into the diner. He gave the ladies a wink.

Pearl clutched her chest and Opal tittered.

I shook my head at him and said in a quiet voice that only his werecougar ears could pick up, "You're going to give them a stroke one of these days." I rolled my eyes. "Do you have a minute to talk?"

He gestured a the mostly empty room. "I'm kind of busy right now."

"You're a laugh riot."

"I have my moments." He turned toward the hallway that led to his office. "Follow me."

"Is Freda off today?" I asked.

"She's helping Lacy move into an apartment." He sighed. "She hasn't been able to find a job that pays decently since losing her legal assistant position with Jock Simmons, so she can't afford the rent on her house anymore."

"That guy needs a butt-whooping," I said with a little too much enthusiasm.

Buzz sat at his desk, and I took the chair in front of it. "What's Jock done now that's got your panties twisted?"

"Something. Nothing. I don't know. Parker got a zoning violation notice today, and Theresa said that Jock's friends with the chair of the zoning board, Clem Hanley." That last name. "Is he related to the kid, James Hanley? The one Addy used to hang out with."

"James is his son." Buzz waved his hand. "But go on with what you were saying."

"Theresa says that Jock has it in for me. He blames me for Theresa leaving him."

"Why?"

"Because he's a delusional jerk, I guess. But anyhow, she says she thinks the violations might be Jock's fault, as a way to get at her and possibly me through the people we care about. And then, after class today, I ran into Ryan. He says he got a citation three weeks ago for a tiny crack in his sidewalk, and that got me thinking—"

"—that what Theresa says might be true." Buzz's green

eyes flared bright under his dark-copper lashes. He bared his teeth as he opened a drawer and pulled out a folded letter. He put it down in front of me. "Mine came in the mail on Friday. They got me for overgrown weeds on that small patch around the signage outside, a downed gutter around the back—which I had no idea was downed because the last time I'd checked it, it was fine—and several cracks in the sidewalk that have been there for years. On top of that, I had a health inspector show up this morning without notice and go through the diner with white gloves. I am extremely cautious when it comes to this place," he said, running his hand through his thick, short curls, "but the guy found a dog chew in the back corner of the kitchen, or so he said."

"Did Smooshie bring it in there? I'm sorry if she got you in trouble."

He shook his head. "I got a good whiff of the half-eaten rawhide knot. It didn't smell like Smooshie."

"So, you think he planted it."

Buzz grimaced then rubbed his palms over his beard. "This wouldn't be the first time I was shaken down by an inspector wanting a small bribe. I'd written it off as such. But Jock is on the town council, and he has a lot of connections. People who don't care that he's a wife-beating son-of-a-bitch."

"If this is him, what's next? I mean, I'd been worried for Theresa where Jock was concerned, but now I'm worried for me and everyone around me." I couldn't meet Buzz's gaze. He'd warned me when I first moved to Moonrise not to get involved with the drama in this town. Keeping my head down was the only way to keep our secret. Instead, I'd involved myself in five murders, and now I'd brought the drama right to Buzz's front door. "I'll figure this out, Buzz. I promise. I'll get Jock off our backs."

"You'll do no such thing, Lily Mason," he said in a scolding tone that reminded me of my father.

My heart clenched, his death from almost twenty years ago suddenly felt fresh, and tears prickled my eyes.

"Don't cry, Lily. I'm not mad at you."

"It's not that," I said. "I just...well, for a second there you made me really miss Dad."

A small smile turned at the corners of Buzz's lips. "I miss him, too." He got up and came around the desk and put his hand on my shoulder. "I'll take care of the Jock Simmons situation if there's anything to take care of. It could just all be a coincidence."

"Do you really think so?"

"No, but I can hope. I'll talk to him man to man."

"What about your rules of engagement?"

At the same time, we both said, "Don't get involved."

"You're my family, Lily, and I will happily come to your aid. Even if it means breaking my number one rule. Besides, you're not the only Mason Jock has a bee up his butt about. After all, I had a pretty public banning of him from The Cat's Meow last year. After he punched Lacy at the hospital, I couldn't let him come around here for lunch and upset Freda. She's been with me for a long time, and like I said, you come to the aid of family." I could see the tension in his body, an itch that needed to be scratched, and I worried that Buzz, maybe, was wound a little too tight.

"Speaking of family stuff. The full moon is on Saturday. You want me to go with you to the state park when you run?"

"I'll let you know."

"Okay," I said. "You know, you have an open invitation to run on my property anytime you want. It really does ease the energy of the moon."

"Changing often makes you careless, Lily. Or at least it does me. I'm choosing to live with humans, so I stay human as much as I can." It was a gentle admonishment of my indiscretions, but an admonishment all the same.

"If you change your mind," I said.

He patted my shoulder and chuckled softly. "Do you want a hamburger to go?"

"Uhm, yes," I said, suddenly hungry. "With everything."

AFTER THIS AFTERNOON, I WAS MENTALLY EXHAUSTED.

Parker was understandably disappointed when I told him I was going home for the night, but he knew what it meant to need to be alone sometimes. He suffered from PTSD from his time of military service, but I had my own demons from battles fought too close to home. And for whatever reason, the day had dug up a pang of sadness in me that I'd thought I'd put away. Letting my inner cougar out to run was the only thing that would help me let go, and I couldn't do that in the middle of town.

Before I left, I'd grabbed a small scoop of Smooshie's poop from Parker's backyard. I dropped the sample off at Ryan's Clinic. While I was there, I looked at the crack in his sidewalk. It was small, like he'd said. Maybe only seven inches long and less than a quarter of an inch wide at its biggest opening.

The minor blemish had been filled with some kind of rubber cement, but a grooved curve near the center of the crack caught my eye. I picked at the filler until just the edge of it came up.

Smooshie circled around me, her leash wrapping my knees and nearly pulling me over. "Hey," I said. "Settle down." I knew she was anxious for a romp in the woods. It had been four days since we'd last been home, and her favorite exercise was chasing my cougar around our ten acres.

"Whatcha doing?" Ryan asked.

"Does this look like a drill hole to you?" I pointed to the rounded spot where I'd picked at the sealant.

Ryan squatted down next to me, and Smooshie lodged her big head under his butt and threw him forward.

"Smoosh!" I admonished on a laugh. "Sorry about that," I told him. "She has no manners."

"It's a good thing she's so pretty then," he said on a chuckle. "Now, let's see what you're talking about." Ryan leaned down closer to get a better look, and I hugged Smooshie's neck, so she wouldn't molest him again. "Maybe. I'm not sure, but it could be. Do you think someone created the crack by drilling into the sidewalk?"

I shrugged. "I'm not sure if it works like that, but after today, I can't help but be suspicious. You might ask the contractor who fixed it what he thinks."

"It's too late to do anything about it now," he said. "If something else happens, I'll pay closer attention."

CHAPTER 4

Tuesday morning, I sat through orientation with a Mr. Phillip Danby for Composition II, and a Professor Dan Charles for my last elective, a botany class. I figured studying plants would give me a leg up when it came to identifying plants toxic to animals, especially after I'd gone on an emergency call with Ryan to a farm where a cow suffered from poisoning after eating leaves from an elderberry bush. It made me want to be more aware of the types of dangers Smooshie might be exposed to out in nature. Besides, it seemed like a fun and easy class, and with two homework-heavy courses already on my short summer schedule, I needed fun and easy.

Professor Charles was younger than I'd expected—tall, thin, and handsome in a bookish way, round glasses, an aquiline nose, and a narrow jaw. Best of all, he seemed excited about plants. My favorite classes were the ones where the teachers were genuinely fond of the subject matter. The syllabus included a field trip day to collect local specimens, which made my nature-loving heart skip a beat.

My phone, on vibrate, buzzed in my backpack, sounding loud in the small classroom. The professor stared down his nose at me but continued talking about what we could expect from the class. I focused on ignoring the droning sound until it stopped. I grimaced apologetically.

"And finally," Professor Charles said, "there are the obligatory classroom conduct rules. One. I won't tolerate tardiness. The door will close and lock at the beginning of class, and I won't open it for late students. You will take an absent for the day."

Harsh, I thought, but okay.

My phone began to vibrate again. I cringed when the professor turned his gaze on me again.

"Two," he said. "I have a no tolerance policy for disrespectful behavior toward me and toward other students in the form of hate speech or violence. If you are a racist, sexist, or any other type of bigot, keep it to yourself, or I will use my discretion to drop you from my class."

There wasn't anything I disagreed with on that policy, and thankfully, my phone stopped buzzing again.

"Third." He held up three fingers. "Cheating in any form will get you failed in this class, and you will be turned in to the administration for discipline."

A young man in the back row snorted. Professor Charles

narrowed his gaze at the student until the kid looked away nervously.

"Fourth. This is a fast-paced class. If you show up, pay attention, and do the lesson plans, you will not only pass this course, you will do it with flying colors. Any failure in this class will be yours, not mine. Any success will also be yours. You're paying to be here, so act like it."

My phone started again. I stifled a groan. Who the hell was calling over and over?

"Fifth." He looked at me pointedly. "Turn off your phones at the door." Then he nodded. "Take your call, Miss Mason. Outside the room." To the rest of the class, he said, "You can go. See you all on Thursday."

I scrambled up and grabbed my backpack. I dug the phone out of the side pocket as I fled the room.

"CRAP." THE CALL DISCONNECTED BEFORE I COULD PICK UP. The screen showed three missed calls from Theresa. I touched the return-call button, and she picked up on the first ring.

"Oh, Lily! Thank heavens. You need to get down to The Cat's Meow right now."

"What's happening?" I was already pulling my keys and running out of the building toward the parking lot.

"I was having lunch with Keith, and Jock came in all full

of piss and vinegar. I think he's drunk. It's not even noon!" Her words were heavy with emotions. "It's so awful! Freda got upset and started yelling, then Jock went off on her, so Buzz got involved. It came to blows, and Buzz knocked Jock to the floor. The sheriff was called. There's a deputy here, taking statements, but Buzz might be arrested!"

"For what?" I dropped my keys when I tried to put them in the truck door. "Shoot." I scooped them off the asphalt.

"He landed the only punch, and Jock wants to press charges. Deputy Morris and Nadine took the call. They're trying to calm everyone down, but I think Buzz needs you. I'm sorry. I'm so sorry for all of this!"

I got the keys in the second time, unlocked the door, and climbed inside. "This isn't your fault, Theresa. Jock is the only one to blame here. Help Buzz as best you can. I'll be there in five minutes."

My heart thrummed in my throat as I threw the truck in gear and ripped out of the parking lot and onto Two Hills Boulevard. Buzz wouldn't normally hit someone, no matter the reason. With the full moon around the corner, he'd be edgier than normal, but he'd managed to keep it civil for over forty years among the humans, so I didn't know why he was suddenly out of control.

I took a deep breath and slowed down. I would be no good to Buzz if I got pulled over on the way to his diner. Still, I drove a little over the speed limit, got a lucky break at two stoplights, and rolled through two stop signs to get to the diner in three minutes flat. Luckily, only one sher-iff's vehicle was in the parking lot, which meant Nadine and Bobby Morris hadn't called for backup.

I parked and raced inside. The diner was full of unusually quiet patrons, all enrapt with the lunchtime show going on between Jock and Buzz.

Jock was giving his statement to Bobby. When I brushed past the two of them, the sweet smell of alcohol clung to the air around Jock. Ugh. Maybe if he got off his liquid diet of booze and ate some solid food, he wouldn't be such a caustic jerk. I doubted it, though. Jock was awful drunk or sober.

His bruised face reddened when he saw me. His speech was slightly slurred as he compared me to a female dog.

"You shut your mouth," Buzz growled, surging forward. He almost knocked down Theresa, who had been standing between him and Jock. Nadine caught one arm. I sidestepped Theresa and grabbed Buzz's other arm. Nadine made little headway hauling him back because, as a Shifter, Buzz was stronger than most men, but I was able to slow him before he could get anywhere near Jock.

"Buzz!" I said with the sharpness of worry. At least his eyes hadn't changed. It would be impossible to explain to a roomful of witnesses why Buzz's eyes glowed if he started to partially shift. "Stop." Between Jock and the lunar cycle, he was about to lose his normal ironclad control.

Nadine's expression reflected my worry. "Let's go to the office where I can take your statement," she said, trying to sound official. When my uncle wouldn't budge, she said, "Damnit, Buzz. I need you to calm down."

He looked at her, and the hardness around his eyes softened.

"You're gonna get yourself arrested if you don't settle down, and since I won't book you, I'll probably get fired. Is that what you want?" she asked, her tone soft with a combination of anger and affection.

"Let's go," I told Buzz. "Back to your office."

"I'm pressing charges, Mason!" Jock said the moment we had Buzz turned and moving in the right direction. "I'll see you behind bars!"

"Keep walking," I said frantically.

When we got him in the office, Freda walked in behind us and closed the door. I could still hear that foul-mouthed ape shouting veiled and not-so-veiled threats.

Freda sagged against the door and wiped her brow with the back of her hand. "That man needs to find Jesus," she said.

Nadine shook her head. "Even Jesus would want to punch that no-good piece of trash."

"Well, I certainly want to punch him," I said, adding my two cents.

Buzz paced back and forth like a caged animal, his rage so strong I could feel it to my bones. I reached out to him, and he flinched away. What was going on with Buzz? It couldn't just be the full moon heightening his agitation.

"Can I have a minute alone with my cousin?" I asked his two allies.

"Sure." Freda nodded to Buzz. "Thanks for having my back out there. I'm just sorry you're in trouble over it."

"He won't be in any trouble," Nadine said. "Count on it." Still, she looked worried. I didn't blame her. He was worrying me as well.

Buzz continued his back and forth stalking even after the two ladies exited. I waited until I could hear them walk away before speaking. "What is going on, Buzz? This isn't you."

He clenched and relaxed his fists several times and rolled his shoulders as if trying to shake an unshakable tension.

"I know the full moon is close, but you've been handling it for years—no, decades. What in the world made you lash out at Jock Simmons, of all people?"

"I hate that man," he finally said, his words edged in a growl. "But I shouldn't have hit him."

"No, you shouldn't have, but I'm more worried about the why than the what. Why did you do it?" I went to the door and locked it then I turned back to Buzz. "You need to shift. Now."

"I can't." He continued his pacing.

I moved in front of him, forcing him to halt. When he met my gaze, I put demand into my question. "Why?"

"Nadine wants a baby."

"What?" It felt as if every gear in my brain started rotating in high gear. "I don't understand. Explain this to me."

"About a year ago, after we moved in together, Nadine started talking about kids."

I took his hands. "But Shifters and humans can't…"

He moved his gaze to our entwined fingers. "Only, maybe they can. I reached out to a network of other integrators living across the country. Four months ago, a guy in California told me he'd successfully impregnated his wife by not shifting at all for six months. He worked with another integrator, a biologist, and found that if a male Shifter withholds his animal side long enough, he creates sperm that carries more human DNA than therianthropic DNA. It becomes compatible with humans."

"You have no idea if any of this is true, Buzz. Why would you jeopardize your life here for something so trivial? Nadine would happily adopt a child if you had simply said you were sterile."

"She wants her own child." He shook his head, then looked at me. "Maybe I want one as well."

I caressed his furry cheek. "Oh, Buzz." I looked around.

"But at what cost? You still have two more months to go, and you are losing it."

"I can do this, Lily. I need to try." The plea of desperation in his eyes made me want to weep.

"What happened to 'we can play with them, but we can't keep them'?"

"I think you and I have both crossed that line."

"The difference is, Parker knows what I am."

He withdrew his hands from mine and turned his back to me. "I can't tell Nadine."

"Why?" Nadine was one of my best friends now, and I'd been tempted more times than I could count to tell her the truth about me. The fact that it was Buzz's secret as well had been the one thing that stopped me.

"I can't risk losing her."

"Don't you think she loves you enough to understand? Parker—"

"Parker has your scent, Lily." His tone was sharp, filled with pain tinged in anger. "I don't have the benefit of a mate scent with Nadine. Your witch ancestry on your mother's side makes you unique."

"Humans fall in love, marry, have babies. All without a mate scent. Sometimes you just have to take a leap of faith."

He snorted. "That's easy for you to say."

I shook my head. "No, it isn't."

"My life isn't up for debate." His eyes flashed bright green.

"You're going to lose it, Buzz." I pointed at the door. "You already have. What are you going to do if you get thrown in jail for assault?"

"I'll be fine." He waved me off. "This is my life. Don't interfere."

"All right." I sighed. "I'll let it be. For now. But you might consider closing shop this week. At least until after the full moon. The fewer people you're around right now, the better."

"I can't close the diner."

"Then get someone else to run it for you. You are a man on the edge of doing something really stupid."

His shoulders slumped, and he nodded. "I'll think about it."

"That's all I ask."

A knock came. "Can I come in?" Nadine asked.

Buzz and I locked gazes. He gave me a nod, so I unlocked the door.

"Am I being arrested?" he asked when Nadine entered.

She smiled. "According to witness statements, Jock threw the first punch." She shrugged. "And while he might not have hit you, it's a clear case of self-defense. Deputy Morris is waiting to see if you want to press charges."

Buzz chuckled. "Tell him to let the douchebag go, but also, remind said douchebag he's banned from The Cat's Meow. For Life."

CHAPTER 5

Parker wore tan coveralls without a shirt as he carried a ladder and a bucket of painting supplies down the sidewalk toward the east side of the shelter. I honked the truck's horn to get his attention and pulled into the driveway. A breeze rustled the leaves in a way that sounded like dry rain.

"You're back early," he said, setting the ladder against the siding.

I shaded my eyes when I got out of the truck. "Class got out early."

Parker greeted me with a kiss that nearly made me forget about my awful morning, while his honey and mint scent made me weak in the knees. "How was it?"

"What?" I asked a little breathlessly.

"Your classes. How'd they go?"

"Quickly. Just a basic syllabus walkthrough in both of them."

He pressed his fingertip between my eyes. "What's this about?"

I moved his hand aside. "Quit poking at my creases."

He put his hands on my hips and gave them a playful twist. "What are you worrying about?"

"Buzz punched Jock Simmons."

"What? When?" He let his hands drop to his sides. "How?"

"Buzz punched Jock. About forty minutes ago. And in the usual way." I made a fist and mocked a punch to his nose.

Parker grinned.

"Don't you dare laugh. It's not funny. He could have gotten into some serious trouble."

"Did he?"

"No. He got lucky. Everyone in the diner told Bobby Morris that Jock tried to hit him first."

Parker laughed. "It couldn't have happened to a nicer guy."

I giggled. "Still not funny."

He held up his hand and made a C with his thumb and forefinger. "Tiny bit?"

I huffed and rolled my eyes. "Fine. It's a tiny bit funny. I really wish I could have seen it happen," I said conspiratorially. "Even so, Buzz is always warning me about drawing too much attention to myself, but he is playing a dangerous game."

"How so?"

We were out in the open with no one around, but it wasn't worth taking a chance that someone might have ears on us. "I can't tell you now." I patted his chest. "Later?"

He nodded. "Over dinner tonight?"

The itch of the coming moon and Buzz's news made me feel raw with broiling energy. I shook my head. "Not tonight. Okay? I think I need to...you know." I made a playful "rawr" sound and shaped my fingers like claws.

"You can always come back later on tonight and put those claws to other uses if you want."

I smirked and smacked his chest. "We'll see." I gestured at the ladder. "Painting the shelter where the paint flaked off?"

"More like scratched off. It looks like someone took a rake to the whole far side."

I frowned. "Maybe this is Jock's doing. He could have hired someone to sabotage the shelter."

"Maybe. Or it could have been a half-dozen people in this town who don't want a dog rescue in Moonrise. We have a lot of support, but we also have a few detractors. I'll just be glad when we can move the operation out to the new shelter."

"Me too. Mostly because we'll be able to save more pit bulls. But also, because it will make you really, really happy, and that makes me happy."

"*You* make me really, really happy."

"Then, I'm content."

A blue mini SUV parked next to my truck. Theresa got out of the driver side, and Keith, who had recently begun shaving his patchy beard, exited from the passenger door. "Oh, Lily!" Theresa gushed. "I'm so sorry about Jock."

"Why? You aren't forcing him to be a complete jackhole. That's a choice he makes all on his own."

"I know, but I did marry him. That choice brought him into my life, and by extension, all of our lives."

"Now, Ther-bear," Keith said. He put a comforting arm around her. "You can't keep blaming yourself."

"I have a feeling he'd be a pimple on the butt of a pig even if you hadn't married him."

Parker added, "Lily and Keith are right. Jock Simmons would find a way to make trouble with or without you in his life."

Theresa smiled but shook her head. "Will you tell Buzz I'm sorry?"

"You're not responsible for the way Jock behaves," I said.

"So, don't be sorry." I forced a smile I didn't feel then glanced up at Parker. "I'm going to relieve Jerry of puppy duty."

"But—" Theresa started, but Parker gave her a quick headshake.

I eyed him suspiciously.

"You go on in. Puppy therapy will ease that crease between your eyes in no time." He gave me a peck on the cheek. "Now, I'm going to fix some code violations, so I don't have to pay an even bigger fine, so I don't start developing creases of my own."

"Har, har," I told him. "Too late."

I followed Theresa and Keith inside but branched off from them when I made a left toward the isolation room. I lightly knocked before entering, my eyes widening when I saw that it wasn't Jerry in the room with the sick baby, but Addison Newton. He'd been away to Southeast Missouri State University in Cape Girardeau since the previous fall.

"Addy! You're here."

The nineteen-year-old, his blond hair a month or two overdue for a haircut, smiled up at me from where he was sitting on a cushion with the pupper. "I just got in last night," he said quietly for the dog's sake. The mangy yearling's ears perked up at my entrance, and his tail swished twice, but that was the only reaction he gave me, content to keep his head on Addy's lap.

I'd known Addy would be home for the summer, and that he'd planned to volunteer, but his early arrival after the day I'd had was a welcome surprise.

"His skin is on fire," Addy said of the dog. "This place renews my faith in people, but it also makes me want to hurt someone."

It was a common emotion amongst the volunteers. We took in some extreme cases of neglect and abuse, and it could make you feel like human beings were the worst. But it was also humans who were doing the rescuing, so the latter couldn't be exclusively true. Bad people existed. It didn't mean all people were bad. The young man comforting and caring for this neglected pit bull was proof that there was so much kindness in the world.

I sighed as some of the tension left my body. "Thank you, Addy."

He gave me a crooked smile. "For what?"

"For being decent."

He chuckled. "You're welcome, I guess."

"So, have you seen CeCe? I heard she'll be home for the summer this week."

He smiled. "Not yet. We've been video chatting every day, and I saw her over Christmas break, but I'm ready to see her in real life."

"I bet." My inner girl squeeed. I was so happy him and CeCe were still making it work.

Addy pet the pup on the head. "You want to take over?" he asked reluctantly.

I shook my head. "It looks like you've got this under control."

"I've missed this place. I've missed the dogs." His eyes crinkled at the corners. "And I've missed you and Parker. It's good to be home."

Addy reminded me so much of my younger brother, a really great kid with some issues. Unlike my brother, Addy had managed to turn his life around. Selfishly, I was glad he'd missed me, but I worried about the sadness in his voice. "Are you okay?"

He stroked his hand down the pup's back and shook his head. "I think I'm just a little homesick."

Theresa came up behind me. "You have a phone call, Lily. Ryan Petry."

"Thanks." I glanced at Addy as Theresa headed back to the office. "We'll talk later."

"Hey, is Jimmy volunteering here now?"

We had a Larry, Jerry, Keith, Jordan, Robyn, Lisa, and a Steve, but no Jimmy. "Who?"

"You know, Jimmy Hanley. He was a buddy of mine in high school."

"James Hanley?" The kid who'd nearly knocked me over the day before. "No. Why?"

"I drove past here last night, and I saw his sports car parked out front. Or maybe it just looked like it."

"I don't think it could have been his. I'll check the roster, but I think our new volunteer Jordan Deeter came in last night."

"Ryan says it's urgent," Theresa said from the end of the hallway.

"Crap." Literally. I'd dropped Smooshie's sample off with Ryan yesterday. What if he'd found something awful? "I've got to go," I said quickly. "Talk soon!"

I closed the door between us and hurried to the office. I picked up the phone. "Hey, Ryan. What's up?"

"Sorry, I tried your cell phone, but it kept going to voice mail."

"It's in my backpack out in the truck. Is something wrong with Smooshie? Did you find anything bad in her stool sample?"

"Some paint chips. I am trying to determine if their might have lead in them. Do you know where Smooshie would have gotten into some old dried paint?"

I had a suspicion. "The shelter siding. Someone scraped the paint off the side of the building. It was one of our zoning code violations."

"Ask Parker if he knows what kind of paint was used."

"What do we do if it's lead paint?"

"You'll need to bring Smooshie in for a complete blood cell count. That will give us a clear indication of whether she's been poisoned or not."

The word poisoned rattled me. "Is this lethal?"

"It can be, but the fact that she's eating and drinking normally is a good sign. Intestinal irritation related to latex or oil paint chips is the most likely culprit, but I just want to make certain."

I waved at Theresa, covering the phone's mic with my palm. "Could you ask Parker if the peeled paint has lead in it?"

"How will he know?" she asked.

"Good question." I took my hand off the mic. "How will we know if it's lead paint?"

"If it's been painted since nineteen seventy-eight, the chances are good it's not lead paint. If Parker isn't sure, bring Smooshie in for the blood test, just to be on the safe side."

"Ask him if it's been painted in his lifetime," I told Theresa. I heard Ryan chuckling. "Hush."

"You're full of charm, Lils."

I giggled. "And you're full of—"

"Now, now," he teased. "Keep it civil."

Theresa came back. "Parker said it isn't lead paint. It's latex."

"Smooshie should be fine then," Ryan said.

"Thanks, Ryan. I appreciate you."

"Aww. I appreciate you, too." He hung up the phone.

My skin buzzed with angry energy. Someone had deliberately scraped paint to make trouble for Parker, and in the process, they almost poisoned my dog.

I glanced at Theresa.

"Everything all right?" she asked. "You look mad enough to spit."

"Do you really think Jock would come after the shelter to get back at you? At me?"

Theresa's voice was soft, her expression haunted. "He likes to punish people." Her fingers absently went to her jaw, a sense-memory of more abusive times. "I don't know if he's the one behind it, but I wouldn't put it past him."

"All right." I gave her elbow a squeeze.

I went outside and found Parker. He painted with the same efficiency he did everything else and was nearly done with the entire side. "What do you think?" he asked when I walked up behind him.

"Looking good," I said.

"You're staring at my butt, aren't you?"

"Maybe." I laughed when he pivoted and kissed me. "You're blocking my view," I told him.

"You saw Addy?"

"I did." I sagged against Parker as he put his arms around me. "It's nice to have him back."

"Are you okay?" He smoothed my unruly hair away from my face.

"Smooshie ate the paint chips that landed on the ground. Whoever did this hurt my girl."

"So, not okay."

"No," I said. "Not okay. I'm just thankful it wasn't toxic. She'll be okay, but now I'm worried. She loves to chew all sorts of things. What if the next thing she tries to eat is poisonous?"

"Smooshie will be all right."

"Promise?"

"I do." He squeezed me tight. "Why don't you stay for dinner tonight? You can go home after."

I nodded. "That sounds nice." The carb-load would help with the calorie burn it took to shift as well. "I'm going to go find Smooshie. I think I need to hug her for a little bit."

"Pull the chicken out of the freezer to thaw. I found a lemon garlic recipe I want to cook for you."

I raised my brows. "You definitely know the way to my heart."

He winked. "I'm no fool."

CHAPTER 6

The lemon garlic chicken had been delicious. I'd eaten every speck of meat off the bones and sucked the marrow from the large ones to avoid discussing why Buzz was acting off kilter. The idea of bringing up the topic of children, when I wasn't sure where Parker stood on the subject, frightened me. We were happy in our little bubble, but if I poked too hard, I knew it could burst. I mean, what if we had opposing views of what a future together meant?

Instead, I'd eaten my right leg full of chicken and mashed potatoes. Which meant, I was extremely full and ready to run it all off. The minute I parked in my driveway and got out of the truck with Smooshie, I stripped down to nothing and casually tossed my clothes inside my trailer.

Smooshie twirled excitedly as she waited for me to get furry. I couldn't wait to stretch my legs. Not being able to have this kind of freedom all the time was the only thing I missed about Paradise Falls. Well, I missed my best friend

Hazel, but she was only a phone call away if I really needed her.

I allowed my cougar to surge forward, feeling her power as my bones and muscles shifted and tawny fur sprouted along my skin. The sensation was better than any high, which is a reason I never understood why some shifters still turned to drugs.

Smooshie and I ran and tussled, occasionally surprise-tackling each other, and offering playful nips at the ears and face. Smooshie loved to play, and she never took the roughhousing too far. I climbed up the side of a large oak, my claws digging in, daring Smooshie to follow. And did she ever. She reached my tail before sliding back down. I laughed, and it came out like a high-pitched scream.

The crunch of gravel on tires and the soft purr of a vehicle motor snatched me from my bliss. I could see headlights coming down my road and turning into my drive.

I jumped down and led Smooshie through the woods toward the trailer. The vehicle had been too quiet for Parker's dually pickup, but it was in the range of Nadine's car. Why would she be here? We hadn't made any plans. And besides, I was pretty sure she'd told me she was working every night this week. Nadine was a deputy for Moonrise, and she'd fallen on the bad side of Sheriff Avery. Honestly, though, I wasn't sure the man had a good side.

I shifted at the tree line where I kept a watertight bag with a change of clothes in it for just such an occasion. I'd been caught one or two times with my pants down, literally, and started stashing clothes near the woods as a precaution.

After I put on the plain T-shirt and pulled up the sweat-pants, neither of which would win me any fashion awards, Smooshie and I had a foot race to the trailer, ending with her inching me out for the win. I laughed—until the overwhelming scent of blood stopped me in my tracks.

I looked at the car. It was a red sports car. Definitely Nadine's. The light in the trailer was on, and the door cracked open. Was she hurt?

"Nadine?" I said as I bounded up the steps. Inside, I saw it wasn't Nadine at all. "Buzz?"

He sat on the couch with the familiarity of someone who'd once owned this trailer, which, until he'd given it to me, he had. His hands were caked in dark, drying blood. That's what I'd smelled. It must have transferred to the door handle when he went in.

"Buzz, are you hurt?"

He looked up at me with a bleak expression I'd never seen on him before. His gaze dropped to the palms of his hands before coming back to me. He shook his head. "I have to leave town. I don't want to go, Lily. I don't. I know I talk about leaving if things get heavy, but I have more to lose now than I ever have in my life."

I knew he was not just talking about the diner and me. He

loved Nadine, even if they weren't mates by shifter standards.

Suddenly, I couldn't stop the sludge of horror creeping into my veins as I asked, "Is it Nadine?"

He shook his head again, and I'll admit I had a brief flash of relief. I tried not to use my witch magic I inherited from an ancient ancestor that compelled people to be truthful with me. Mostly, I thought it wasn't fair to folks who wanted to keep their secrets secret. Even so, the magic did make people open up if they wanted me to know the truth even when I wasn't trying.

In this situation, though, I needed to know what happened to Buzz, so I sat beside him on my small couch and put my hand on his arm, careful to not touch the blood and pressed him for an answer. "Then who, Buzz? Tell me what happened."

He blinked at me for a moment then said, "Jock Simmons is dead."

I centered myself with some deep breaths as I walked to the fridge and pulled out a cold cola. "Here," I said, as I popped the tab and set it on the small side table nearest Buzz. "Take a sip and tell me everything."

He squeezed his eyes shut as one-hundred kinds of pain played on his face. He pressed his palm against a watery eye. "Damn it. I had it. I really had it this time."

I sat down next to him. Smooshie, after lapping up half her bowl of water, jumped up onto the couch and placed herself behind me. She pressed her wet nose and mouth against my arm. I turned my attention to Buzz. "Had what?"

"A home. Someone to love. A life."

"Oh, Buzz." I understood his feelings. They mirrored my own when it came to Moonrise. "Talk to me. We can figure this out. Together."

Buzz shook his head. "I threatened him. There were witnesses."

"This afternoon when you punched him?"

"No. Later. I was still agitated after I closed the diner at four, so I went to his office. I didn't mean it. I just wanted to scare him enough to get him off your back." He tapped his forehead with his fist three times. "I can't believe I broke my first rule. It was so stupid. Such a stupid move."

He might believe he'd gone after Jock for me, but I think the full moon and his not shifting were huge factors in his risk-taking. Hitting him with the hard truth now, though, wouldn't do a thing to make the situation better. It was tantamount to an "I told you so," and I liked to think I wasn't that kind of person.

"Where is Jock now?" I asked.

"At the diner. In the parking lot."

"Is he still there?"

Buzz looked up at me, his stare sharp and full of intensity.

"I got a call from the police saying that someone reported a break-in at the diner, so I went over there. I found Jock lying on the sidewalk in front of the door. He was alive." He held out his hands as if to show me the blood. "Barely. But…I tried. I tried to save him. I was too late. Then there were sirens. And lights. I panicked. I ran."

"What about the break-in?"

"I don't know. I got out of there as soon as I heard the police coming."

"And you left your truck in the parking lot."

He nodded.

"And you made it to your place and got Nadine's keys and drove here."

He nodded again.

My thoughts tracked in multiple directions. Some practical. Some impractical. But the impractical ones weren't helpful, so I pushed them aside. "Was Jock conscious when you found him?"

"Yes."

"Did he say anything?"

"Like who stabbed him in the stomach?"

"That would be a start."

"No such luck. He was mumbling "ah-knee" or some such nonsense. He was frothing at the mouth, and the word sounded mushed. Then it sounded like he said, "hand," so I thought it might be a clue. Like he grabbed something from the person who'd done it, but I checked, and other than his wedding band, I couldn't find anything on or in his hands." Buzz's eyes grew distant. "His heart was beating so fast. His breathing slow and gurgly. Then he died."

"Did the police see you?"

"I don't think so. But my truck is sitting in the parking lot with the keys in it. I don't think it's going to be a stretch for the sheriff to pin this on me."

"You think he'll railroad you?"

"You don't? With his daughter in the middle of a messy divorce with the dead guy? Sheriff Avery is going to be pointing the finger at any target that points away from Theresa."

"Theresa wouldn't kill Jock."

"Not my point."

I sighed. "I know. But, hey, you got me and Nadine on your side. You know neither one of us will let you go down without a fight."

He scrubbed his face again with his palms. "What am I going to tell Nadine?"

"Did you try calling her?"

"My phone's in the truck with my keys. I barely got the

truck in park before I saw Jock on the ground. I hopped out and tried to help him. Why didn't I just put the truck in reverse and leave."

I squeezed his forearm. "Because you're a good man." I got up. Smooshie spread out on the cushion. I raised my brow at her. She wagged her tail as if to say, move your feet, lose your seat. I shook my head and grabbed my phone from the pile of clothes I'd left on the floor.

"What are you doing?"

"I'm calling Nadine."

He looked as if he would protest for a second, then bowed his head and nodded.

I opened my contact list and touched Nadine's avatar. She was sticking out her tongue and flipping me off. We'd laughed when I took the picture.

The phone rang once, and Nadine picked up. I could hear voices in the background

"Hey, Dad," she said. "What's up? Is Mom okay?"

"Deputy Booth, who are you talking to?" I heard Sheriff Avery ask.

"My dad. I'm sorry. My mom's sick with the flu and Dad took her to the doctor this afternoon. I'll tell him I'll call him back."

"Personal calls on personal time," he groused, then his

tone softened. "And tell Jen I hope she gets to feeling better."

"You got it," she said. Then more quietly, she said, "Did you get that, Dad?"

"Yep," I replied. "Buzz is here. He's with me at the trailer. He didn't do this."

"I never believed he did," she said, but her voice was shaky.

"How does it look for Buzz?"

"Not going to lie," she said. "It doesn't look good." The background noise had grown distant, so I could tell Nadine had walked away from the crowd of cops, para-medics, and whoever else happened to be on the scene.

"Buzz said he got a call from the police saying there had been a break-in at The Cat's Meow. Do you know who called that in?"

"I haven't heard there was a burglary-in-progress call. We arrived on an anonymous tip."

"Can you check? Maybe Jock startled whoever tried to break in, and they killed him."

"I've been told I can't have any part of this case, but I won't sit idly by while my guy gets railroaded."

I wrung the bottom of her T-shirt, stretching the hem until it curled. "Don't put yourself in jeapordy."

"I'm not the one you need to worry about. They've

already sent some uniforms over to our house to search the place. I'm afraid your place will be the next stop. You have to get him somewhere safe, at least for tonight. We can make a plan tomorrow."

"No," Buzz said. "I don't want Nadine involved on the wrong side of this. Her career is important to her."

"Tell him I heard that, and he is more important to me than some badge."

"Deputy Booth!" the sheriff shouted.

"I got to go. Tell him… Tell him I love him."

Before I could respond, she hung up.

I glanced at Buzz. "You heard her, right?"

"She's going to blow up her world for me." He banged the bottom of his fist against the arm of the sofa, an action that sent Smooshie scrambling off the couch and tucking in behind me.

I knelt next to my girl and made a soothing sound as I scratched her head.

"I'm sorry," Buzz said. "I didn't mean to startle Smooshie. I just don't want Nadine to ruin her life for me."

I directed my gaze at Buzz. "That's what you do when you love someone."

He stood up and staggered as if his legs were made of liquid, cussing the five steps it took to get to the door.

"Where are you going?"

"To turn myself in?"

My eyes widened. "Why?"

"Because," he said, with a glint in his eye. "That's what you do when you love someone."

"What are you going to tell them?"

"The truth, and I'm going to hope they don't crucify me with it."

"Do you want me to go with you?"

"I don't want to involve you any more than I already have."

"You're my family," I told him. "I'm involved."

Buzz forced a smile at me. "If you want to help, you can find me a decent lawyer. Preferably alive."

I snorted a laugh, mostly to keep from crying. Jock might have been a good lawyer, but I'm not sure he'd ever been decent. "I'll start making some calls."

CHAPTER 7

I picked up my cellphone and called Parker. He picked up on the first ring.

"Hey, Lils. This is a nice surprise. Are you coming over?"

"Yes." I wanted to blurt out what was happening, but my fear for Buzz stole my words.

"What's going on?" Parker asked when I didn't say more.

"Do you...do you..." I took a deep breath. "I need a lawyer."

"Why?"

"Jock Simmons is dead."

His tone sharpened. "Have you been arrested?"

"No." I clutched my phone. "Not me. Buzz is turning himself in. He needs a good lawyer, and I just don't know any."

"Buzz killed Jock?"

"No." This time my tone sharpened. "He was there when Jock died, and he ran when the police arrived."

"I can see how that could be seen as suspicious."

"But he didn't do it," I added rapidly. The phone slipped out of my shaking hand. Smooshie yipped a bark as it whacked her head. "Oh! I'm sorry, girl." I scrubbed one hand on my pants to dry it and grabbed the phone. With my other hand, I rubbed Smooshie where the device had dented her noggin. "I'm so sorry!"

"Is she okay?"

"Yes. I dropped my stupid phone on her."

"Pack a bag, and you and Smoosh get on over here. I'll start making calls and see who I can find for Buzz."

While I am normally a decisive, independent woman and not a lot gets me flustered, the idea of losing Buzz, whether he went to jail or, later, decided to run away, scared me stupid. So, when Parker took charge of the situation, I gratefully let him. "I'll be over soon."

I drove with the windows down, allowing the cooler night air to wash over me. Smooshie stuck her big head out the passenger window, her tongue flapping in the breeze.

Between the wind and the sound of the engine, I finally managed to quiet the panicked thoughts crowding my head. I had to find a way to help Buzz and finding him a lawyer wasn't it. My specialty lay in my ability to sniff out clues, question suspects, and find killers. Real killers. I needed to pull myself together and be the niece Buzz deserved. One who would fight to keep him out of jail at any cost, not the one who falls apart at the idea of losing, again, another family member.

My lungs felt congested with grief as I thought about everyone I'd lost. Mom, dad, brother...Buzz was the only relative I had left in this world.

I fumbled in my bag and grabbed my phone. I opened the screen, touched my contacts, and made the call I should have made ten minutes earlier.

"Is he safe?" Nadine asked when she answered the phone.

"He's on his way to the sheriff's station," I answered. "He doesn't want to run or hide."

"Dammit, Buzz," Nadine hissed. "This looks really bad, Lily. I'm afraid if Buzz is arrested, the sheriff will find a way to force the case closed."

"We won't let him," I said. "Parker is finding him a lawyer. Are you still at the crime scene?"

"No. The sheriff sent me off to patrol so the other deputies would be free to process the parking lot."

"Did they call in Reggie, yet?" Reggie, or rather, Regina Crawford, M.D., was a family practice doc here in Moonrise, and she was also a certified medical examiner. She also happened to put the dream in our BFF Dream Team.

"Yes, she was coming when I was going. I didn't get a chance to talk to her."

"How long do you think the scene will be covered?"

"You mean how long before everyone leaves."

"Exactly."

"Probably two more hours."

"Crap."

"But—and I mean, I would never advise you to enter an active crime scene—but I can't tell you how many family members have shown up out of nowhere. It's not hard to imagine a cousin who happens to drive by, seeing a bunch of lights and sirens and stops out of sheer worry. You know, if you get caught."

"Good. It's a plan. What about you?"

"I'm going to the station. There is no way I'm going to let them railroad Buzz through processing. I'm staying with him until his lawyer arrives."

I flipped my right blinker on, turned onto Main Street, and headed into town. "I'm about five minutes at the most from the diner. I'll text you later."

"Lily, I don't know what I'm going to do if…"

"We'll make sure you don't have to figure it out," I said with more confidence than I felt. "Give Buzz a hug for me." I hung up. I couldn't believe I was heading to the scene of a murder. Willingly. This would be the fifth one since I'd moved to Moonrise, a town steeped in secrets and intrigue. The sheriff already disliked me.

I glanced at Smooshie. "At least we didn't discover this body, right?" It would be hard for Avery to blame me this time, but I'm sure, under the right circumstances, he'd find a way.

I saw the flashes of red and blue when I was a block away. I rolled the windows up on the truck until Smooshie could only poke her nose out as I parked across the street from the diner. For half a second, I considered letting Smooshie out to cause a distraction, but the idea was bad on so many levels. First, having a massive pit bull running into a crime scene full of police officers would scare them and possibly get my baby killed. Secondly, see the first reason. Smooshie was a lover not a fighter, like most of her breed, but their reputations in the media painted a more dangerous picture.

I scratched her ear. "Sorry, girl. You're going to have to wait here for me." When I got out of the car, she moved over to occupy the driver's seat. "I won't be long." Especially since I expected to get kicked out as soon as the sheriff saw me. Two deputy vehicles, one ambulance, Buzz's truck, and Reggie's black sedan formed a semicircle near the street side of the diner's parking lot. A wall to prevent onlookers from getting too big of an eyeful.

A group of about ten people had gathered on the south end, some with phones out and pointed at the diner. The news of Jock's death would be big talk in Moonrise.

My stomach knotted. This would be all over the news and social media, and in this age of guilty until proven innocent, everyone would believe Buzz was a murderer. The thought put more determination into my step as I walked toward the ambulance since it was the closest to Buzz's truck, and that meant, the closest to the body.

"Get those rubberneckers out of here," I heard the sheriff yell. "We're not selling tickets to the show." His voice was higher than normal and strained.

"We're trying," I heard someone say.

Good. The sheriff was distracted, opening an opportunity for me to sneak right in. I pressed my back against the side of the ambulance and inched toward the front.

"What are you doing?" a woman asked.

I jumped and spun at the same time, startled that anyone had managed to catch me off guard. Robyn Pattersen, the paramedic who had taken care of me last year when I'd been exposed to carbon monoxide, sat in the driver's seat of the ambulance with the window down. We'd become friendly, and a couple months later, she'd started volunteering, along with her partner, Steve, at the rescue.

I clutched my chest, waiting for the anxiety to release. "I didn't see you there," I said.

She chuckled. "Obviously." She pointed at her extensive setup of side-view mirrors on the rig. "But I saw you."

"Are you going to tell the sheriff?"

"Not if I don't have to," she said. "I'm just waiting on the doc to give me the thumbs-up to take the body to the hospital morgue. There's no hurry at this point."

"Did you see him?"

"Simmons?" she asked.

I nodded.

"Yes. Steve and I were first on the scene with the police. After we determined he was deceased, we were told to wait until after Doctor Crawford arrived." She pointed toward the other side of the cab. "Steve is waiting out there." She looked at me, her brown eyes soft. "I prefer living patients."

I gestured to the step at the base of the door. "May I?"

"Sure," she said. "I won't tell if you don't."

I grabbed the door and pulled myself up and looked past Robyn toward the scene. Paramedic Steve stood with his arms crossed over his chest while Reggie knelt beside Jock's body. I felt the blood leave my face.

"You better sit," Robyn said. "You look like you're about to pass out."

I gulped as a wooziness took hold. "That's unexpected."

"Death has a way of taking hold."

It wasn't death, though. I'd seen plenty in my lifetime. It could be that I'd just seen him this afternoon, alive and spitting nails. "It's strange seeing someone you know like that," I said. "Even when that someone is Jock Simmons."

"He hit on me once at Dally's Bar," Robyn said. "He hadn't even bothered to take off his wedding ring." She shook her head and patted her tight curls. "And I wasn't the only one. He was a real piece of work."

I gave her that knowing smile that passes between women sometimes. "That's a nice way to put it." I peered past her again. Reggie was standing now, and she was talking to the sheriff. I tuned out everything else and allowed my cougar to surge the tiniest of bits to the surface as I stretched my hearing to listen in.

"A single stab wound to the right upper abdominal area, a few centimeters below the ribs. I can't say for certain about the weapon, but the incision is right at two centimeters and clean, almost surgical. I'll have a better notion of depth when I get him to the morgue for the autopsy.

"Get on it tonight," he ordered. "I want a cause of death on my desk in the morning."

"I plan to do the preliminary autopsy tonight, Sheriff. But I can't promise a cause of death by morning."

"A blind man can see he was stabbed."

"A blind man can also see that there isn't much blood."

The sheriff's expression soured. He narrowed his gaze at

Reggie, one that said, "I'm an imposing man. Don't mess with me."

Reggie rolled her eyes. "I'll do what I can do, Sheriff Avery."

"How long ago did Jock die?" he asked her.

"There's no livor mortis, so under two hours, by my estimation," she told him.

Livor mortis was when gravity settled blood into the lowest areas of a deceased body. Since Jock was face up, the discoloration would have happened in his back, buttocks, thighs, and heels.

"Did the stab wound kill him?"

"On the surface evidence alone, I'd say, maybe. But the blood volume doesn't indicate exsanguination."

So, there wasn't a lot of blood. Not enough for the loss to kill him. Maybe the knife had nicked an organ, or the bleeding had been mostly internal.

The sheriff's voice grew quieter as he moved closer to Reggie. I leaned in, closing my eyes and stretching my senses even fuirther.

"I know you are friends with Nadine and that Mason girl," Sheriff Avery said.

"So?" Reggie responded.

"Just a reminder to do your job," he told her.

"And I know this man is your soon-to-be ex-son-in-law, a guy who abused your daughter and has slept with a dozen women in town. So, maybe we both need a reminder," Reggie hissed.

I smiled at her fierceness.

"What are you doing?" Robyn asked.

I opened my eyes and turned my head. Our faces were inches apart. This close, I could see a tiny pox scar near her nose. In other words, way too close for friendly acquaintances. "I'm so sorry." I backed my head out of the opening. "I felt a little faint for a moment," I lied.

"It looked like you were thinking about pooping. You were making the *I'm-full-of-it* face."

I giggled. I'd seen Smooshie get that face once or twice daily. "Thanks for letting me have a look. I better get going."

Robyn nodded. "I hope things turn out okay for your cousin."

"Me too."

CHAPTER 8

Smooshie didn't make a peep when I climbed into the driver seat, forcing her to take a position on the passenger side again. Her tail wagged hard enough to break glass though, so I gave her a quick, scruffy petting around the neck and head. "Such a good girl. A good, good girl." I patted the seat. "Now, settle down."

My phone, which I'd left on the seat, had five missed calls. Whoops. I hadn't told Parker I was going to make a detour. One of the calls was from Nadine. That's the one I returned first because I wanted to know what was happening with Buzz.

"Hey, Nadine. What do you know new?"

"The sheriff isn't back, yet, but he told the on-duty, Jack Davenport, to start processing Buzz for arrest. This is so stupid, Lils! Buzz is a good man. He's not a murderer. I know it in my bones."

"I agree," I said. "We're going to fix this. Where's Buzz now?"

"They took him down for fingerprinting. The sheriff has banned me from the case. He told Jack to arrest me if I so much as put a foot inside the in-processing area. Right now, the only place I want to put my foot is up an old pompous prick's rear end."

"Nadine!" I snorted a laugh. "Hang in there. I'm on my way to Parker's, and we'll make sure Buzz has a lawyer. He knows not to say anything to anyone without representation."

"I wish you were here," she said. "I could sure use the hand-holding. Maybe even a Smooshie cuddle or two."

Smooshie, hearing her name, shoved her nose next to my ear and tried to lick the phone. I gently nudged her with my elbow. "Smooshie is sending you all kinds of kisses. If you want me to come down there, I'll drop off the baby with Parker and head over."

Nadine sighed. "Don't. There's nothing you can do. Heck, there's nothing I can do. I feel so freaking helpless."

"Buzz loves you, and he knows you're on his side. That's plenty."

"I hope you're right," she said. "Tell me again."

"It's going to be all right. We'll fix this."

"I believe you."

"Good. Because it's the truth." I really wished I felt as confident as I sounded. I put the phone down after I hung up. I was only a few blocks from Parker's house, and it was quicker to drive there than to call him back.

I knocked on Parker's door before letting myself in. He'd told me many times it wasn't necessary, but I hadn't been able to break the habit. Smooshie took off in a run, skittering into the kitchen where Parker kept the bowls for food and water for both dogs. I heard her loudly lapping up water from the other room, and if I knew my girl, she'd started in Elvis' dish first. She liked to eat his food and drink his water whenever he wasn't around, tricky girl.

"Parker?" I put my keys and bag down, checked the kitchen and the bedroom, the bathroom door was open. Elvis, on his long legs, came trotting out from the utility room. I gave his face a cuddle. "Where's your man?" I asked him. Over the past year, I'd noticed Parker needing Elvis less and less for his PTSD. He said that having me around kept him calm, but he still took Elvis most places.

I returned to the front door and took my phone from my bag. I opened it straight to my voice mail, clicked on the first of two messages, and put the cellphone to my ear.

"Hey, I got a lawyer, Loretta White, to take Buzz's case. She is driving from Cape Girardeau, so she won't be able to meet him at the sheriff's station for an hour or so. A buddy of mine vouched for her. I'm sorry I can't—"

The message cut off. I clicked on the second one.

He spoke faster this time. "Hey, again. Anyhow, the Blakes called about Hester tonight. She'd started vomiting followed by tremors, and they said she started walking wobbly until she just flopped down. They are taking her over to Ryan's clinic, and I'm going to meet them there. I'm really sorry that I'm not home for you, but I know you understand. Love you, and I'll be home as soon as I can."

Veronica and Mick Blake were one of our best foster families. They'd taken in Hester, a geriatric seventy-five-pound brindle, a month ago. The elderly dogs were harder to get adopted, and we counted on people like Veronica and Mick to give them a loving home until we could find a permanent place for them. Ryan had given Hester a clean bill of health, so I couldn't imagine what had happened for her to suddenly take ill.

I called him back, and he answered on the first ring. "Hi," he answered. "I'm sorry I'm not there."

"I'm glad you're with Hester. She needs you more than I do right now, and I'm sure Mick and Veronica are scared, too. How is Hester doing?"

"Ryan took some blood and hooked her up to an IV. He's doing a few tests, but he thinks she ingested some antifreeze."

"How?"

"The Blakes don't know. Mick says he doesn't have any at

their house." I could hear the anger edging his tone. "Which means Hester was probably poisoned deliberately."

Elvis nudged his head up under my armpit as if he could sense the growing agitation in his master, even from miles away. I could hear Parker's breathing as I walked to the couch and sat down. I breathed with him. Elvis took up two of the cushions to the right of me with his massive size, and Smooshie squeezed in between the armrest and my leg on the remaining cushion. "I'm sorry, Parker. That's awful. Some people are really terrible. Does Ryan think she'll be okay?"

"He's optimistic, but it's a matter of wait and see."

"Like most things in life." I wedged the phone between my shoulder and ear to free up my hands to pet the dogs. "I miss you."

"I miss you, too." He sighed. "Keep the bed warm for me."

"You got it." When I hung up, a cloud of stench surrounded me. I looked from one dog to the other, both of whom didn't acknowledge the stinky butt in the room. "Rude."

IT WAS MIDNIGHT WHEN MY PHONE LIT UP WITH A TEXT. I'D fallen asleep on the couch, sandwiched between two furry heaters. It was from Nadine. *Buzz has been arrested. Court at 9:00 a.m.*

"Son of a witch's britches." I texted back. *Are they holding him? What about bail?*

He might not get bail because of the seriousness of the crime. Lawyer is going to try.

I let out a frustrated growl, and both dogs got up and moved away from me. "I'm sorry," I told them. To Nadine, I texted, *I'll be there.*

I heard the key in the door before it opened. Parker pulled his wallet from his back pocket, set it down with his keys on the stand near the entrance.

I whistled to get his attention. His tired eyes brightened when he saw me.

"I was trying to be quiet. Didn't want to wake you," he said.

"It wasn't you," I told him. I held up my phone. "Nadine texted. Buzz has been officially charged."

"What does that mean for him?"

"It means Sheriff Avery isn't going to waste resources trying to find the real killer. He won't want anyone looking too hard in his family's direction."

Parker sat next to me and laced his fingers with mine. "Do you really think Theresa killed Jock?"

"I wouldn't think so, but people can surprise you." After all, my mom and dad had been killed by my best friend's mother. "I'd like to rule her out."

"Do you have class tomorrow?"

"No. I'm supposed to work at the animal clinic in the morning, but Buzz has court, so I'm going to call in." I hated to give up the money. Ryan paid me $15.25 an hour, almost double the minimum wage in Missouri, but I only worked on Wednesday mornings and Thursday afternoons for a total of eight hours. Parker paid me minimum wage at $8.60 per hour, and I only worked twenty paid hours a week for him as an employee. The rest of the time at the shelter, I volunteered. The twenty hours was all Parker could afford and keep the place running, so I didn't mind. I loved working with him to save as many Smooshies as we could. If only love could pay my bills. I sighed and rested my head on Parker's shoulder. "Do you think Theresa will come in tomorrow?" She worked most Wednesdays.

"I haven't heard from her. If she doesn't show up at seven, I'll call her. If she does come in, I'll go to court with you."

I squeezed his hand and inhaled his scent. "You always make me feel better."

He leaned his cheek against the top of my head. "I feel the same."

"Nadine and Buzz want to have a kid," I said.

Parker's heartbeat accelerated, and his chest rose once and held for a count of three seconds. "Really?" he finally asked.

"Yep."

"I thought that wasn't possible between, you know…"

"Shifters and humans?"

He rubbed his throat. "Yes, that."

"Buzz said a guy on the West Coast managed to make it happen by suppressing his animal side until his swimmers—"

"Lost their tails?" Parker let out an unexpected snort.

I smacked him playfully. "That's not funny."

"It kind of is."

"It kind of is," I conceded. "But, yes, essentially, it caused a receding in our therianthrope DNA that allowed the guy to get his wife pregnant."

"How did he do it?"

"By not shifting for six months."

Parker leaned forward and rotated his hips to face me. "Isn't that dangerous? I know I don't know everything about your people, but I remember you telling me how the full moon is hard to walk away from. Could that have made Buzz…unsettled enough to kill Jock?"

"Honestly, it could. And he hasn't shifted in four months, which has turned him into a powder keg. His whole life has been about restraint, yet, he'd punched Jock today in front of a diner full of lunch customers. But my witchy lie detector didn't ping at all when he told me he didn't kill the man. I know he's innocent."

"It doesn't ping with me. You told me that it's because we're mates and that supernatural bond doesn't allow you to use your magic on me. Do you think because you and Buzz are kin that it might not work on him?"

I shook my head. "I've caught him in a fib or two. Believe me, it works."

"So, a kid, huh?"

"That's the goal, as long as he's not spending his life in prison or on the run."

"Do you want my opinion?"

"Sure."

"I think Buzz needs to be honest with Nadine about who and what he is if he intends to have children with her. It's not fair to Nadine, regardless of Buzz's good intentions."

"You're right," I agreed. However, I didn't want the conversation turning toward us and babies, so I leaned into Parker and kissed him. He met my lips with gentle enthusiasm.

"Is this your way of changing the conversation?"

I stared into his intense blue eyes. "Take me to bed, handsome."

He stood up and held out his hand. I took it. He helped me from the couch, then surprisingly caveman-like, he picked me up and threw me over his shoulder. I let out a delighted laugh as he hastily made his way down the hall.

CHAPTER 9

"I think the entire town of Moonrise is sitting in this courtroom," I said to Nadine. We'd arrived early on Wednesday morning, but it was standing room only. I spotted Opal and Pearl Dixon sitting on the defense side, four rows back from where Buzz sat with his lawyer, a middle-aged blonde woman in a severe dark-blue dress suit. It had to be the criminal lawyer, Loretta White, from Cape Girardeau.

Opal saw me and waved. She scooted away from Pearl and indicated for Nadine and me to come sit by them.

"There," I said to Nadine, pointing in their direction. "The sisters have saved us seats."

Theresa had called off work early in the morning, which meant Parker had needed to stay at the rescue. Ryan calling us to say he wanted to keep an eye on Hester for a few days, but that she would make a full recovery, was the one bright spot of the morning.

"What if the judge doesn't grant him bail?" Nadine asked. "What if Buzz has to stay in jail until the trial?"

"I wish I knew," I told her.

"Buzz is in trouble," Opal said. "Judge Robinson is a hard case. He's as close to a hanging judge you're going to get in these parts."

"How do you know this?" I asked.

"We like to come watch the criminal cases," Pearl answered. When I raised a brow at her, she added, "It's the only amusement I'm allowed these days."

"All right," I said. "So, tell me about this judge."

"He rotates in every six weeks, and he rarely sets bail, and when he does, it's higher than most people can afford."

Buzz turned to look at me.

"You doing okay?" I asked softly.

He nodded, but the darkness under his eyes told another story. He wouldn't survive prison. And with the full moon only four nights away, I wasn't sure if he could take another night in county lockup. "Hang in there."

His eyes pivoted to Nadine. The look he gave her, mate scent or no mate scent, said he loved Nadine Booth with every part of himself. I held her hand when her lower lip began to tremble. When she saw Sheriff Avery walk up the aisle, Nadine's back stiffened and her face hardened. She stared straight ahead.

I, on the other hand, studied the room. Maybe the real killer had come to see his or her handiwork.

Freda and her daughter Lacy stood in the back. Lacy had reason to want Jock dead. He'd sexually harassed her when she was in his employ, and when she pushed back, he'd attacked her. Without her job at the law office, she'd had to move herself and her son into a smaller place. Still, murder seemed like a stretch. I didn't see Lacy as the revenge type. Theresa sat with her mother, Anna Avery, across the aisle near the middle. Theresa's eyes were red. She'd cried. For Jock? I guessed it was possible, even after everything he'd put her through, that she might still love him.

I shook my head. More likely, her pregnancy hormones were steering her mood. Still, I wouldn't completely rule her out.

An attractive dark-haired woman wearing a gray v-neck sweater blew her nose and pocketed the tissue. The question was, did she suffer from seasonal allergies, or was she upset? I'd gotten better at guessing human age, and I estimated she was in her thirties, mid to late. "Who is that?" I asked Nadine.

"I have no idea."

"That's Electa Laverty. She and Jock were doing the nasty flamingo." The veins bulged in Pearl's thin hands when she made a circle with the thumb and fingers of her left hand and poked the circle with her right index finger in a suggestive manner.

"Pearl!" Opal smacked her sister's hands down to her lap. "Stop that."

"Are you sure you didn't make up the rumor?" I asked, reminding her that I knew she was the poisoned pen who'd nearly sent me running from Moonrise before I'd even gotten settled.

Pearl grinned. "I saw them kissing in his car some months back. They were definitely doing it."

Electa's name sounded familiar, but I couldn't place her face. Still, I added her to my list of suspects.

Who else? I scanned the room again. The number of bodies packed in the court had increased the temperature in the room by ten degrees. I ran hot by virtue of my species, but the heat combined with the claustrophobia settling in was making it hard to concentrate. I settled on Sheriff Avery. He'd have heard about Buzz's dust-up with Jock yesterday. Maybe he'd used it as an opportunity to get rid of his no-good son-in-law. Maybe it had been an accident, a crime of opportunity. Still, stabbing Jock at one place then dumping his body somewhere else had been a risk. A calculated one. Someone smart like Sheriff Avery might have thought it was worth the chance to deflect blame. He could have disguised his voice and called Buzz about the break-in at the diner. All he'd have to do then is show up like he'd come to investigate the scene like everyone else.

"The call," I said aloud.

"What?" Nadine asked.

"Someone from the police called Buzz last night and sent him over to the diner. That person was probably the real killer. Did they confiscate his phone?"

Nadine nodded. "He told them in the interview about the call, but no one will tell me if the call exists or not. The sheriff has forbidden anyone from talking to me about Buzz's case."

I glanced at Avery again. "Do you think someone at the station deleted the call?"

"No." She shook her head, then nodded. "I don't know. Maybe. If Buzz says he got a call, he got one. It should have been on his phone log."

I glanced around again. It was hard to see everyone, but there were a lot of faces I recognized, mostly as regulars at The Cat's Meow.

"Buzz has a lot of fans here," Opal said as if reading my mind. "No one wants to see him stitched up for this."

I smiled at the old woman. "Thanks."

"Outside each other," Pearl added, "Buzz is the closest thing we have to family. We don't want to see him done dirty. If you need anything at all. You tell us, and we'll do our best to help."

They both spent almost every afternoon at the diner. They saw who came and who went, and they were privy to private conversations because people tended to ignore the elderly. This made them huge assets in my book. I nodded to the sisters. "I'll take you up on that."

Opal flushed with pleasure, and Pearl smiled. We still had a few minutes before court started, so I stood up for a better look around. Addy Newton was there with his parents. Jordan Deeter and James Hanley were together against the wall under one of the large picture windows. So, maybe Addy *had* seen James' vehicle at the shelter two nights ago. I'd have to talk to Jordan about allowing unauthorized people in the kennel area.

"All rise," a bailiff called out.

Nadine and the Dixon sisters stood up next to me as everyone in the courtroom came to their feet.

"The Moonrise county court is now in session. The honorable Judge David Robinson presiding."

A silver-haired man, probably in his sixties and wearing a black robe, walked out of an adjacent room and strolled up the steps to his bench. His lips were thin and set in a grim line as he adjusted his glasses up his nose before saying, "Be seated."

We all sat. At least those of us with seats.

The judge took notice. "This is a courtroom of the law, not a party. Anyone standing with no official business here in the court needs to leave now."

A general rumble of complaints and outrage made its way through the crowd.

The judge banged his gavel. "Anyone still standing in this courtroom in thirty seconds will be arrested and held for not less than one night in the county jail for contempt. One. Two…"

By the time he got to three, people were running each other over to get out. I could see why Pearl had called him a hard case. I could also see why she and Opal enjoyed attending court during his rotation. However, having him as my uncle's judge made me anxious.

By the time the thirty seconds were up, the courtroom, emptied by half, had quieted exponentially.

The judge nodded his satisfaction. "Will the defendant please rise?"

My uncle and his lawyer stood up.

The judge read from a file. "Mr. Daniel Mason, you have been charged with second-degree murder and fleeing the scene of a crime. How do you plea?"

"Not guilty, your honor," Buzz said.

The judge didn't even look up. "Recommendations?"

The prosecuting attorney, a pinched-looking bald man, said, "Due to the brutal nature of the crime, your honor, the county of Moonrise requests bail be denied." He ended on a confident smile. And why not, he'd gotten the hanging judge.

Even so, I wanted to wipe the confident, smug smile off his confident, stupid, smug face.

"Your honor," Ms. White protested. "Daniel Mason is a pillar of this community. He owns his own business, is in a committed relationship, and he has family ties here in Moonrise. He has no criminal history. For heaven's sake, he's never even had a speeding ticket. There is no evidence he is a flight risk or a danger to this community, which are the only reasons to deny bail."

"I agree," the judge said.

"Thank you, your—" The prosecuting attorney's mouth dropped open. "Excuse me?"

"You heard me, Mr. Nichols," the judge said. "Ms. White has made a good case for bail, and I'm inclined to grant it." Ms. White looked nearly as surprised as Mr. Nichols.

Pearl nudged me with her elbow. "Me thinks somebody got laid last night."

My eyes widened as I shushed her. I scooted forward, Nadine chewed her thumbnail, and it felt as if the whole court was holding its breath while we waited for a number.

"I am setting bail in the amount of one-hundred thousand dollars. The trial is set six weeks from today. Mr. Mason, you are to stay in Moonrise for the duration of your pre-trial. You will not be allowed to possess any firearms during this time. If you fail to show up on your assigned court date, you will lose your bond money, and you will be held for the entirety of the trial until you are either cleared of the charges or convicted. Do I make myself clear."

Ms. White nudged my uncle. "Yes, your honor," Buzz replied.

It took every ounce of self-control not to jump up in the air and whoop.

Nadine, who'd done a great job of holding it together, wasn't so restrained. She rose to her feet and gripped the back of the bench in front of us, her arms and legs shaking from the adrenaline that flooded her body.

I got up to steady her. "He's coming home," I said gently. "Buzz is coming home."

CHAPTER 10

I left the courthouse feeling slightly more optimistic— but only slightly. Buzz getting bail granted was still a long way from clearing his name. If the turnout in the courtroom had been any indication, there would be a lot of folks with strong opinions making themselves heard over the next six weeks. I planned to work nonstop to find the real killer because the alternative was too horrible to think about.

I needed to know how Jock died, and there was only one person who could supply that information.

I called Reggie Crawford.

"Hello, Lily," a girl who was not Reggie answered.

"CeCe!" I exclaimed. "When did you get into town?"

"This morning."

"I can't wait to hear all about your classes, but right now I need to talk to your mom. Is she around?"

"No, Mom was up all night, so she took the morning off to sleep. I came in to help Mrs. Trevors call her patients and reschedule appointments."

"Why do you have her phone?"

"Oh, that. Well, Mom knew you would call. She told me to tell you that Sheriff Avery warned her that if she talked to you at all about the case, he would report her to the medical board for standards of practice violation. She doesn't trust herself not to spill the beans if she talks to you, so she made me take her phone so that I could be the bearer of bad news."

"Oh, well…crap. I don't want to get her in trouble."

"Mom said to tell you that she's sorry."

"Tell her she's got nothing to be sorry for."

"I will. Also, can you pick me up at her office?"

"Didn't you drive there?"

"Car trouble." She didn't elaborate.

If I couldn't talk to Reggie, Theresa was next on my list. I needed to know if she was responsible for Jock's death, and if she wasn't, she still might be able to fill in the blanks on who in this town hated the man enough or had any kind of motive to kill him.

"I have a full morning. Why don't you call Addy? He's back home for summer break."

"No," CeCe replied swiftly.

"Is there a problem between you two?"

"No," she chuckled. "Nothing like that. I just want to surprise him tonight is all. So, I really need *you* to come get me." She emphasized the word "you."

"Me specifically."

"Yes," she said.

"Okay. I'm on my way."

Reggie's office was in a strip mall that housed an insurance company and a physical therapist practice. Her clinic was the first door as you pulled into the parking lot. Since she wasn't seeing patients until this afternoon, her side of the lot only had two vehicles, one I assumed was CeCe's, but neither of them looked old enough to have broken down.

I expected CeCe to be waiting outside for me. She wasn't. I pulled into a space near the entrance and parked. I waited a minute, and when CeCe didn't come outside, I texted. *I'm here.*

Not quite done. Can you come in?

K, I replied.

I'll admit I was annoyed as I got out of the truck and stomped inside. Sherry Trevors, a middle-aged office manager, with professionally dyed and highlighted brunette hair and abnormally peach skin from too much tanning, smiled up at me. "You can go on back," she said.

"Thanks." I passed three empty exam rooms to get to Reggie's lair, as I liked to call it. CeCe stood behind her mom's desk and waved me inside. "Hey, Lily." She wore her raven-black hair straight and down past her shoulders, and she wore a powder-blue scooped-neck tee that complemented her pale skin and a pair of blue denim skinny jeans.

"You look good, CeCe. Washington University agrees with you."

If possible, she appeared both pleased and sad. "I really like it there. My biochemistry classes are challenging but fun."

I arched a brow. "Biochemistry sounds like a laugh riot."

She shook her head on a laugh. "I really want to be an ecologist, and this is a good major to start with."

Ah, youth. I loved that she wanted to save the world one plastic bottle at a time. "I'm proud of you." I nodded at the computer. "Are you ready to go?"

She tapped some paperwork on the desk. "Not just yet."

"What do you have left to do?"

She tapped the paperwork again, and I noticed the sheet of paper under her hand. At the top, it said Office of County Medical Examiner Investigation Report. "Mom says she's awfully sorry she can't help you on this one. Especially since Buzz is involved." CeCe flicked her gaze from the paper to me and back. There'd been no need, though. I might have been a little dense earlier, but now the message came through loud and clear.

Reggie had arranged for me to "accidentally" come upon the report, so that if she was called before the medical board, she could say, without perjuring herself, that she didn't tell me anything about the autopsy.

"I'm just going to run to the bathroom before you take me home," CeCe said. "I'll meet you outside."

I slid the paper toward me after she left the room and moved right to the nitty-gritty.

Body presents with left-sided periorbital and maxillary hematoma.

In other words, the black eye Buzz had given him. Nothing ground-shaking there.

Dried sputum, slight pink tinge around mouth.

Pink? That indicated blood. Buzz had said Jock was slurring his words and frothing at the mouth.

Unusual waffle pattern hematomas to bilateral patellas.

Bruised knees. The next was the interesting part for me.

Stab wound to right upper quadrant of abdomen. Weapon was a thin blade. Clean incision edge indicates an extremely sharp tool. Gastrointestinal perforation of the stomach and small intestines. No other signs of incision trauma.

The knifing would have been extremely painful and possibly fatal without treatment, but the blade had not nicked an artery so it would not have been enough to kill him in a hurry.

Excessive fluid in both lungs. No scarring to indicate a history of lung disease.

It would have been difficult for Jock to breathe, let alone talk. No wonder his words had been slurred.

Crystals found in kidneys, bilaterally, signs of acute renal failure. Crystals sent to lab for further testing.

Ouch. Kidney stones were no joke.

Fatty liver with mild cirrhosis. Blood chemistry pending.

Most likely from his long-term use of alcohol. Jock liked his vodka, and he had been drunk when Buzz punched him at the diner.

And finally, cause of death. *Acute Pulmonary Edema, cause unknown. Cannot rule out homicide until further tests are completed.*

He'd suffocated on the fluids in his lungs. It sounded like the knife wound hadn't killed him, even if Buzz had stabbed Jock, which was potentially good news. They might get him for assault, but murder was a stretch. Even so, the court might consider that the knife wound contributed to the death even if he didn't bleed out.

I jotted down a few notes on copier paper then slid the report back into its folder. I heaved a sigh that had nothing to do with relief. I had more information now, but I still didn't have a clue.

When I went out to the parking lot, CeCe stood next to my truck with a set of keys in her hands. There was a woman leaving the dentist office at the same moment. CeCe said loudly, "The car's working now, Lily. It must have been something electrical." She winked. "I'm sorry you wasted a trip."

"Seeing my favorite niece is never a wasted trip." I smiled and gave her a hug. "Thank you. Have fun tonight with Addy."

AFTER I LEFT THE PLAZA, I CALLED THERESA. SHE'D surprised me by telling me she was at home. Not the trailer where she'd been living with Keith for the past year, but the house she'd shared with Jock.

I've seen many faces of grief in my lifetime, but Theresa's confused me. She'd hated the man. He'd abused her mentally and physically for years. He'd made the past year of her life a virtual nightmare, yet, she'd been teary-eyed in the courtroom, and now she was sitting in the home where most of her abuse had been perpetrated. I couldn't decide if this made her seem less guilty or more so. Either way, I wouldn't know until I asked.

The address was 417 Oyster Lane in the Moonrise Heights

suburb, the richest neighborhood in Moonrise, complete with its own clubhouse and golf course. Dang, the lawns all looked as if they were unrolled fresh daily, and I could fit my trailer and my house into most of their garages.

When I rolled up to Theresa's place, I actually found myself gasping a little at the grandeur. She had a huge circle drive with a three-car garage, a cobblestone path crossed the yard, and the edges were planted with a variety of blue, yellow, and purple perennials. The actual house was modern in design, two-story brick-front home with an entryway made for giants, and high, steep gable roofs that appeared to be sectioned, giving the place a definite mansion vibe.

I'd never been in this part of town before, and I knew without a shadow of a doubt, I would only ever be a visitor here. This was where the one percent lived, and I was confident that unless I hit the lottery, I'd never be able to afford one of their vehicles, let alone their homes. Even if I could, the neighborhood, even with its glorious landscaping, left me feeling cold. I'd dealt with the wealthy in my hometown, and whether the rich were witches, shifters, or humans, they almost always had one thing in common: they believed they were inherently better because they had money. At least that had been my belief, but Theresa had never made me feel like I was less than, and this had been her life. I liked to think of myself as an open person, someone who gives people the benefit of the doubt, but I supposed even I could make assumptions about a group of people based on my limited experience.

Still, I didn't think I'd be joining the Moonrise Country Club anytime soon.

I parked on the street, because my truck Martha tended to leak oil and old transmission fluid, and I didn't want to mar the perfect gray of the concrete driveway. I felt jittery as I strolled to the front door. I knew Theresa, I reminded myself. She was my friend, and I would keep reminding myself, even if she had been the one to kill her husband.

I rang the doorbell. Theresa's voice came over an intercom and said, "Come in, Lily." The door made an electronic clicking noise as it unlocked. I opened it and went inside.

"Hello?" The open floor plan included a huge kitchen with high-end appliances, a ten-foot breakfast bar, and floor-to-ceiling cabinets. Her living room had a large brown leather pit set, with matching leather ottoman, a moose skin in front of the fireplace, and several deer head and fish mounted on the walls. Had Jock been a hunter? He struck me as the kind of guy who only preyed on women, but maybe he had a taste for conquest in other areas as well. The one thing missing from the large space was Theresa. I spoke loudly, "Theresa, where are you?"

"I'm upstairs," she yelled, her voice strained and hoarse.

I walked the half spiral up to the second floor and followed the banister down a wide path past several closed doors until I came to an open one. Theresa sat on a four-poster king-size bed, complete with down comforter and enough pillows to build a really good fort. There were four suitcases on the floor with women's dresses, shirts, jeans, and more haphazardly piled inside each open case. Theresa squinted up at me, her eyes still red and slightly swollen. Her hands were on her thighs, palms up. She glanced down at them and back at me.

"When I left him, I took nothing. I came to get my clothes." She sounded like a lost child.

"Do you need help packing?"

She shuddered as a sob choked from her throat. Tears flowed down her cheeks, and the noise she made reminded me of a hyena. Goddess. She was crying, but she was also…laughing.

"Theresa? Are you okay?"

"He's gone," she said. "Really gone. And I'm…" She laughed more, the tears still rolling. "I'm so relieved." She stared at me, horrified at herself as the words left her mouth. "Jock is dead, and I'm free. I don't have to be afraid ever again."

CHAPTER 11

I thought the idea of never being afraid again was a bit overly optimistic. However, I knew what she meant. Jock couldn't hurt her anymore. Not physically, anyhow. I sent up a prayer to the Goddess that Theresa hadn't had anything to do with Jock's demise. If she had, as far as I'm concerned, it was justified, but the law wouldn't see it in that light. And I wouldn't let my uncle go to jail for her.

"I'm glad Buzz got bail this morning. All I wanted to do in that courtroom was to stand up and tell everyone that we should be thanking him, not trying to convict him. Getting rid of Jock was a community service."

"You loved him once," I said.

Her expression turned stony as she focused her gaze on me. "Any love I felt for him, he beat out of me a long time ago." She put her hand on her stomach. "Keith is ten times the man Jock ever was. A hundred times."

"Do you really think Buzz killed Jock?"

Her brows lifted. "Don't you?"

"No. I think he was set up."

"By who?"

"You tell me?"

"Lily, you don't think I had anything to do with this, do you?"

"No, I really don't, but you understand, I have to ask. Did you kill Jock or have him killed?" I put my mojo into the question. It didn't always work, especially if the truth was something the person planned to take to the grave. Theresa, who hated secrets even though she had many, had been susceptible to my truth magic in the past even when I wasn't trying.

Surprisingly, though, this time she didn't answer me. "I have to pack my things. Keith is expecting me home."

I could have probably forced her to answer my question, but in doing so, I'd ruin any relationship we had. I still didn't think she was a killer, but maybe she was protecting someone. Her dad? Keith? Maybe. I would find another way that didn't require me to destroy Jock's biggest victim in order to get justice.

"Okay," I said. "Do you want me to help you?"

"No. I'm not even sure I want any of these things. I don't know why I came back here. I've been living in Walmart clothes for the past year, and I've never been happier. Maybe I will give everything to Goodwill."

"You know this is your house again? The divorce wasn't final, so you should inherit everything." Which was also a huge motive. I hadn't realized how much Theresa had lost until I came here today.

"It is," she said as if just realizing. Her eyes shimmered with emotion. "What am I supposed to do with that?"

I shook my head. "Nothing. At least, not today." I put my hand on top of hers. "When the time comes, I'm sure you'll figure it out."

She must have changed her mind because she said, "I think I'd like it if you stayed to help me finish here."

"Then, I will." And as much as I wanted to help my friend, this was also an opportunity to search for more clues.

Forty minutes into folding, packing, and loading, I'd discovered that Theresa had a shoe collection that rivaled Carrie from *Sex and the City*. Most of the shoes were three to four inches high, and my feet had ached just looking at them.

"Do you want something to drink?" I asked Theresa. "Surely Jock has soda or something in the fridge."

"He doesn't allow beverages in the bedroom," she said automatically.

Gently, I replied, "He doesn't make the rules anymore."

"Right," she said. "Yes, then. I'll take juice or ice water. I'm trying to be more aware of what I'm putting in my body."

I nodded and smiled. "I'll find you something."

I'd passed the kitchen on the way in, so I knew exactly where I was going, but I made a few detours on the way there, trying to find Jock's home office. It was on the first floor past a formal dining room, a bathroom, a guest bedroom, and a library full of legal books. The office was hexagonal with taupe walls, chocolate trim. A dark walnut desk in front of a large window overlooked an impressively gaudy fountain using a replica of Michelangelo's *Bacchus* sculpture, and the water had been rigged to flow over the wine goblet in the party god's hand as little sprays of water jumped playfully about his feet.

His office space was entirely too tidy. I stretched my cougar sense, inhaling deeply. Jock's scent was faint. Barely there. If he used this office at all, it had not been recently. He didn't have a computer on the desk, which meant he probably used a laptop. I'd seen him with one at his office. I'd call Nadine later and see if it had been confiscated. Had the police searched his law office? Would they, since the crime hadn't taken place there, and they were certain they'd arrested the right person? I was itching to drive over right now, afraid to let any evidence that could clear Buzz slip from my grasp.

The lack of scent in the office was strange, but okay, Jock could have done most of his work at the office. But I realized, I hadn't smelled much in the master bedroom either. Had Jock been staying somewhere else? The house didn't have any dust in it, so obviously he had a housekeeper, but there was nothing personal in the place. Nothing to indicate it was someone's home.

I went to the fridge. Inside was a case of flavored sparkling water, some cranberry juice, two bottles of top-shelf vodka, a fancy cheese wheel, Champagne, wilted lettuce, a small jar of coarse ground mustard, and an expired gallon of milk.

"Where have you been, Jock?" I asked out loud.

"I'd heard he'd been seeing someone," Theresa said.

I'd been so focused on the fridge, I hadn't heard her come downstairs.

She smiled. "Did you find something to drink?"

"Sparkling water and cranberry juice."

She made a face. "I'm not in the mood for either of those."

"What are you in the mood for?"

"A shot of whiskey." She laughed. "Even in death, that man makes me want to drink." She put her hand on her stomach again. "All I ever wanted was a man who would look at me the way my dad looks at my mom. He calls her Hummingbird because when they met in college, she was the busiest girl he'd ever met." Theresa smiled. "Mom was on the student council, she belonged to Beta Gamma Sigma, an honor society for business students, and she played college volleyball all while carrying a full class load. He used to joke that if he hadn't put out honeysuckle to trap her, his hummingbird would have flown right past him." She sighed. "Why couldn't Jock have been that guy? I'm thirty-five, Lily. Is that too old to be a mom?"

"Of course not. Thirty-five is the new twenty-five. Meghan Markle is thirty-seven, and she's having a baby. Heck, lots of women are having babies in their late forties now."

"I was pregnant once when I was twenty-three. Jock and I had only been married a year, and he was just getting his practice established." Her face blanched as she recalled the memory. "When I told him, he left the house without saying a word. That night was the first time he hit me. He'd accused me of scheming behind his back." She shuddered.

"What happened?"

"I went and had an abortion the next week." I could feel the pain in her words. "I told him I'd miscarried. I knew, the first time he'd laid hands on me, that I would never be a parent. It was something I'd wanted for as long as I can remember, but Jock…"

"Was a pig," I finished for her. "You deserve better. I'm glad you're with someone who makes you feel special. Loved." I still didn't know if Parker wanted kids. What if we didn't want the same things? Would that be a deal breaker? "And Keith is happy about the pregnancy?"

"Over the moon." She beamed with pleasure as she said

the words. "He's already talking baby names, turning the second bedroom into a baby room, and getting safety locks for all the cabinets and covers for the outlets. He's going to be such a good dad."

Keith's compassion with the rescue dogs left me with little doubt he'd be spectacular as a father. "Any child would be lucky to have you both."

Impulsively, Theresa hugged me. She was taller, so I got a face full of breasts. When she let me go, she said, "Thank you, Lily. You always know how to make me feel better."

"It's my pleasure."

"I'm sorry about earlier. I didn't kill Jock, and I don't know who did."

My lie-o-meter lightly pinged, which meant she probably didn't know for certain, but might have suspicions. "Who would want him dead? Can you give me a few names?"

"Lots of people disliked Jock, but killing someone, that takes some real hate."

"Revenge, greed, opportunity, accident, jealousy, pleasure, and mental illness."

"What?" she asked.

"The reasons people kill. It doesn't have to be about hating him." I decided to try a different approach. "Tell me if any of these names jump out at you as someone who might have a motive. Electa Laverty?"

"Electa? No. She'd do anything for Jock. They have been friends since high school."

"Interesting. How about James Hanley?" I didn't really think the kid had a real connection to Jock, but he'd been in the courtroom and at the rescue. I had a gut feeling he'd done the damage to our siding, creating the paint chips that had made Smooshie sick. Even if he wasn't a killer, I planned to execute a little old school Shifter justice for the young man if I found out he was responsible. And no, that didn't involve me actually executing him, but I would make him sorry.

"James? Clem's son?" She shook her head. "Jock was James' godfather. He and Clem go back to high school as well. Jock didn't want any children, but he had been fond of James."

Okay. Strike two.

"Do you have anyone else?"

Her dad and her boyfriend, but I didn't think it prudent to ask about them. "No. I don't suppose I could have the keys to Jock's law office."

"Lily!"

"I'm just kidding." But not really.

"Well, even if you weren't, I don't have the keys."

Shoot. I guess I was going to have to figure out some late-night breaking and entering. "I better get going," I told Theresa. "If you need anything at all, you give me a call.

And I'll cover your shifts at the shelter until you are ready to come back."

"I think I'm ready," she said. "I miss the furbabies already." She stopped me at the door. "If I hear anything that can clear your cousin, I promise to tell you."

Again, she wasn't being dishonest, but the statement made enough noise in my head that I knew she would tell me the truth as long as it didn't cost her. I couldn't blame her. There are not a lot of good reasons to lie, but protecting the people you love, that one ranked right up there.

CHAPTER 12

"Smooshie!" I squealed with complete delight as she greeted me at Parker's front door, rearing up on her back legs, turning in circles, and wagging her whole booty with excitement. "Someone wants to play." I rubbed her jowls between my hands and kissed the top of her nose. She lifted her head at the same moment, knocking against my chin and making me bite my tongue. "Ow." Even though it hurt, I laughed. "My bad." After the day I'd had, along with the tragic revelations about Theresa, it felt good to be with my girl.

She gave me a *rue, rue, roof!* bark followed with a playful growl. "I missed you, too."

Smooshie tap danced around me as if to say, I don't understand English, but I'm willing to play along.

I'm sure Parker had kept himself busy this morning. Sitting around doing nothing was not his strong suit. He had wanted to be at the bail hearing with me, but I'd insisted he stay at the rescue. Between Theresa being gone and the new intake, the shelter had needed him more.

I grabbed Smooshie's leash from the coat hooks near the entrance. I held it up. "You want to go for a walk?"

She jumped up and twisted like an actual bull and barked with joyous fervor. I laughed again. "You are so silly. Get over here." When she came, I held up two fingers and said, "Sit." She sat. I held up four fingers and said, "Stay." She couldn't hold her tail still, and her butt gyrated against the floor. "Gah! Why you got to be so cute?" I asked her. I clipped her leash onto her collar. "Such a pretty girl. A pretty, pretty princess."

I grabbed some poop bags then led Smooshie out the front. A bumblebee zipped past her head, and she nipped at the air it had occupied. "Don't eat the bee," I told her as we walked down the sidewalk. We stopped into the shelter first so I could see Parker. As much as I calmed him, he did the same for me.

I'd expected to see him in the office, but Keith Porter was there instead. He'd shaved his patchy beard but still dressed as if he were going to the skate park. He yawned and rubbed his face, the lines around his young eyes deepening with exhaustion.

"You should have taken the day off," I told him.

He jumped a little. "You startled me. I didn't hear you come in.

"I'm sure Parker would have found someone to take your hours. You know, so you could be with Theresa."

He shook his head. "Her dad said it wouldn't look good if I showed up to court this morning." He frowned. "Did you see her?"

"Yes. She's getting a few things from her house that she couldn't take when she'd left him." Smooshie whined a little. I petted her head and made a soft shushing sound.

"When her mom called last night, Theresa dissolved into tears."

"So, you were both home when you were called about Jock's death?"

"Yes. Theresa hadn't been feeling well, so she was napping at the time."

Which meant, Keith could have left their trailer, found Jock, stabbed him, and put him in Buzz's parking lot. It would have been a lot to plan, and a bit of luck would have had to come into play, but it wasn't impossible. "Had she been napping long?"

"About an hour." Keith narrowed his eyes on me suspiciously. "Are you trying to figure out if I have an alibi?"

"No." I gave him a frank stare, then said, "Maybe."

He snorted a bark of a laugh. "I'm flattered you'd think I'm capable. I wished Jock dead plenty of times, but I didn't kill him."

His confession rang true, but I couldn't stop thinking about something Theresa had told me after she'd finally gotten the nerve to leave Jock. "Theresa once said that she'd been afraid to tell you about Jock's abuse because you were the kind of guy noble enough to do something about it."

"Noble enough to do something stupid" had been her exact words.

"And I might have, had she stayed with him. But she left him and came back to me. I wouldn't do anything to jeopardize that. I love Theresa more than I hated Jock." He smiled grimly. "That's a ton of love, let me tell you. Theresa isn't the kind of person who could kill someone, and I'm not either."

Buzz was being framed, and as much as I liked Keith and Theresa, and believe me, I thought they were both awesome, I knew that sometimes good people could be driven to do terrible things, especially under the right circumstances. Smooshie whined again. I scratched her ear. "Hold on, girl. We'll go out in a minute." I just had one more question I wanted to ask Keith.

Parker's sweet, minty scent preceded him into the room. His arms wrapped my waist, and he placed his chin on my shoulder. I let him hold me for a moment, before I said, "Hey, you."

"Hey, you," he said back. "How'd it go this morning?"

"The judge gave Buzz bail. The Dixon sisters said he was

tough and rarely favored the defendants. I really thought he would hold Buzz until trial."

"Who was it?" Keith asked. "The judge, I mean?"

"Judge Robinson."

Keith nodded. "His wife divorced him two years ago. Jock Simmons represented her in the matter, and the judge ended up with a raw deal. I'm surprised he didn't let Buzz go on his own recognizance."

"How in the world do you know this?"

"My mom works for the county clerk, and she's old school Ozarkian."

I raised a questioning brow.

"She likes her gossip," he explained. "I really am sorry for Buzz, whether he did or didn't kill Jock." To Parker, he said, "I have to get to work, but I'm going to go give Marvel some cuddles before I go." Keith worked at the auto parts store on West Central Street. He usually worked afternoons until closing, but occasionally he had morning shifts. Even with a full-time job, he never missed his volunteer hours.

Parker stood up straight. "Thanks for coming in this morning. I know you would have liked to have been with Theresa instead, but I really needed the help."

"No, problem," Keith said. "I was happy to do it."

"Who's Marvel?"

"The new puppers," Keith said. "The little guy needed a name, and I think he's a little marvel, so we gave him the name. He's so stinking cute."

Uh-oh. Someone had been bitten by the love bug. I had a feeling that once the dog came through his mange treatment and neutering, he was going to find a forever home in Keith's double-wide trailer. "That's a great name," I told him. "Hey, before you go, did the police ask you for an alibi? You or Theresa?"

"No, not really, but I just assumed since Buzz was caught in the act—"

"He wasn't," I interrupted. "Buzz found Jock alive. He tried to save him."

"That's not what we were told," Keith said.

My hackles rose. "Since Buzz was gone before the police arrived, I think it's safe to say that none of them actually saw what happened."

"But Theresa's mom said there was a witness?"

This was the first I'd heard of someone else being at the scene. "Who?"

"I don't know, Lily. Honestly, that's all she told me."

"I'll figure it out. You go get you some of that puppy," I told him.

"You're leaving to find out who the witness is, aren't you?" Parker asked as he turned me in his arms.

I stared up into his baby blues. "You betcha."

A pungent aroma filled the room. I glanced over at Smooshie, who'd been really quiet. She smiled up at me, her tongue lolling out of the side of her mouth as she panted happily. "Oh, poop," I said.

"What?" Parker asked.

"Poop. Literally." I pointed to a brown pile of doggy-do on the floor behind Smooshie. I couldn't be unhappy with her. I mean, she'd tried to tell me a couple of times, but I'd been too busy trying to squeeze information from Keith. "Sorry, Smooshie. My bad."

Parker chuckled. "It's not the first time or the last time this floor will be crapped on. I'll get it cleaned up if you want to go on."

"Now, how in the world did I manage to land such a fine man? You cook and clean. It's like I hit the lottery." I went up on my tiptoes and gave him a peck on the cheek. "I'll make it up to you later."

"Dad's invited us to dinner tonight. You up for it?"

"Will this be a double date?" I teased. Reggie and Greer had been dating for a year now, and while Parker liked Reggie and was glad his dad wasn't alone, it unsettled him that I knew a lot of details about his father's sex life. BFFs talk. It's a thing.

"I wouldn't call it that, but yes, Reggie will be there."

"Yes," I said a little too eagerly. Reggie might not be able to talk to me about the case, but it didn't mean she couldn't answer a few generic questions I had, like, how does someone go about dying of acute pulmonary edema? Because if the knife wound hadn't killed Jock, then whatever had caused his lungs to fill with fluid had. "It's a date."

CHAPTER 13

At six-thirty in the evening, Parker and I arrived at Greer's house. The interior had changed a little over the past twelve months. The velour beige and blue flowery couch had been replaced with a pale-green loveseat. Greer had put away most of the pictures of Parker's mom. She'd died when he was in high school, and they both missed her, but it was awkward trying to date when there were signs all over the place that you weren't ready to move on from your past. Reggie had insisted that he keep the family portraits up, but the wedding photos were gone. He'd also changed the curtains to something more masculine and less frilly. He'd asked Reggie's opinion. She'd told him to go with something that reflected his own personal style, to which Greer had replied, he had none.

Nadine and I enjoyed Reggie's dating stories. She'd been in a messy marriage before we'd all met. Her ex-husband had tried to cause a lot of trouble for her, which is how she and CeCe had ended up in Moonrise.

Greer, a handsome man with blue eyes and graying hair, hugged me at the door. Smooshie shoved herself between my knees to get to him. Greer laughed when she nudged his leg with her nose. He let me go and reached down to pet her. "Hey, girl. It's about time you showed up. I only invited your mommy so I could see you."

Greer often babysat Smooshie for me, and they'd developed a close bond. Next to me and Parker, Greer was her favorite person in the whole world. He said it had to do with personal charisma, but I think the treats he kept tucked in his bill drawer were a determining factor as well. Smooshie was not above being bribed. She might as well have hung a sign around her neck that said, "Will kiss and cuddle for chewies."

"It's good to see you, Greer."

"It's been a month of Sundays since we've had a sit-down," he said. "I've missed you."

Between the shelter, the Petry's Pet Clinic, and school, I had a full plate, but it was no excuse to drop Smooshie and run. "I'll make time. Promise."

"How's Buzz holding up?"

"As expected."

"Hey, Dad," Parker said, he and Elvis bringing up the

rear. He held out a bag. "I brought the wine you asked for."

"Great. Put it in the fridge to chill." He closed the door behind us.

"Where's Reggie?" I asked.

Greer shrugged. "She's running a little late. Some work came up. You don't mind waiting, do you?"

"Nope." Parker walked to the love seat near Greer's recliner and sat down. "It will give us a chance to catch up."

"How's the work on the new place coming along?" Greer asked. "I keep meaning to get out there and take a gander, but there never seems to be enough time."

Parker's face lit up as he spoke about the new shelter. "The main shelter building is completed. It has turned out better than I could have imagined. It has twenty large kennels, four isolation rooms, three playrooms for volunteers and dogs to hang out, a bathroom with a large shower, a utility room with an industrial-sized washer and two dryers that we got dirt cheap. A large office with two bunks, just in case someone has to stay overnight. I have to go out there this weekend and finish putting the fences up for the eight different outdoor spaces. I rented an augur last week and drilled all the holes and then set poles in concrete."

Happiness wound through me as I watched him talk about the work with so much pride. His passion for rescuing pit bulls was a true calling. I admired his tireless efforts.

"One of our volunteers, Jordan Deeter, is a graphic art major at the college. She did some wonderful mural work in the playrooms. She's also done a great job revamping the website." I pulled out my phone and clicked on the gallery so Greer could scroll the pictures.

"Wow, you've done some incredible work here, Parker." He glanced at me. "You, too, Lily. I know my boy is capable of doing this on his own, but he wouldn't have gotten this far in such a short amount of time without you."

I blushed. "Parker deserves all the credit." A year and a half ago, we had found a sack of stolen bank cash on my property. Parker and I had nearly lost our lives to two men who'd been searching for the money for a long time. After they were arrested, I split the reward money with Parker. Seventy-five thousand dollars each. I'd used the money to pay off my house and get started on fixing it, and Parker had used his half to get the foundation poured for the new shelter, and the entire structure roughed in and roofed. Those were the most expensive items. He'd spent the last year and a half begging for donations of time, materials, and money to finish the place. "His tenacity, hard work, and never-quit attitude got the place built."

"I'm proud of you, son," Greer said.

Parker grinned. "It's going to be amazing, Dad. As soon

as we get all the paperwork in order, we're going to plan a big open house in a week and a half on Saturday. Hopefully, it will get us some more foster families and volunteers. If we're lucky, we'll get a few dogs adopted in the process."

"You know I'll be there, and I'll help out however I can."

The handle rattled then the door swung open as Reggie walked in. "Hello," she said. "Sorry I'm late."

I could see Parker's thoughts in the myriad of expressions playing on his face. He was having mixed feelings about Reggie walking into his Dad's house without knocking first. Her black hair was pulled back in a severe bun for work, and she wore a gray pinstripe suit that had been tailored to fit her body beautifully. She finished off the ensemble with an onyx necklace and earrings with black heels as accessories. She appeared as a powerful woman ready to take on the world, and I loved that she was my friend.

I took Parker's hand and squeezed it. It was okay for him to have feelings about Reggie filling the void his mother had left in Greer's life, but I was grateful he wasn't petty enough to act on childish emotions.

I jumped up from the love seat when she crossed the room to me. "Lils!"

"Reg!" We embraced. "CeCe looks so good. College life is agreeing with her."

"I know, right?" Reggie said. "I can't believe she's moved

on from all black. I never thought I'd see the day." She smiled at Parker. "It's so nice to see you, Parker. Lily tells me you all are almost done with your new shelter and ready for the grand opening. That's really exciting."

"Yep," he said. "We're excited." He forced a smile.

Greer stood and gave Reggie a kiss. Nothing too sexy, but it was tender enough to make Parker glance away. I, on the other hand, watched, because for one, it was lovely, and second, my heart was bursting with joy for my friends. Their happiness made me happy.

"Are we ready to eat?" Greer said.

"Starved," Reggie said.

Greer grinned as he took Reggie by the hand, and they walked to the kitchen.

I held my hand out to Parker. "Are you ready to eat?"

He took it, and I helped him to his feet. "I think I've lost my appetite."

"Don't be a spoilsport."

He kissed me. "Never."

~

AFTER DINNER, PARKER AND GREER CLEARED THE TABLE AND started the dishes while Reggie and I went out to the front porch to "get some air."

Reggie kicked her heels off when she sat down on the porch swing. "Antifreeze," she said.

"What about it?"

"Antifreeze can do a lot of damage to a body."

"We had a dog poisoned just last night," I said. "She's okay. Ryan says she'll make a full recovery because it was caught within five hours of ingestion."

"That's great, Lily." She crossed her right leg across her knee and turned to me. "It's awful the things it can do in a body. Hypothetically, it can cause confusion, diarrhea, crystals of calcium oxalate can form in the kidneys causing renal failure, and—"

"—it can cause pulmonary edema," I guessed. It was clear we were talking about Jock Simmons.

Reggie nodded. "Terrible way to die."

"Hypothetically," I added.

She shrugged. "Hypothetically."

"How long would it take to die, hypothetically?"

"Well, it depends on the amount of antifreeze and the overall health of the individual. Calcium oxalate crystals form in the kidneys in two to three days. That causes acute kidney failure, but even then, if it's caught early enough, they can live with dialysis, medication, or transplants. Pulmonary edema is rarer, but it can manifest in some victims if they already have the beginnings of lung disease, and they've been dosed for a week or so."

"Wouldn't the person taste the antifreeze?"

"It's sweet, so it's easy to hide in sweet stuff."

"But this is all just hypothetical," I added.

"Exactly," Reggie said.

So, whoever killed Jock had been poisoning him over a short period of time. Who would have had access to his meals or his drinks? A bartender or waitress, for sure. But they risked someone else possibly ingesting the antifreeze. Jock hadn't spent much time at home lately. The lack of his scent in the house was enough for me to come to that conclusion, but he'd had to stay somewhere. I mean, the guy wouldn't have slept in his car. Pearl and Opal had said they'd seen him kissing that woman from the courthouse a few weeks ago. Had Jock been staying at her house?"

"I don't suppose you know an Electa Laverty?" I asked Reggie.

"It's an odd name," she said, shaking her head. "Odd enough that I'd remember if I had."

The screen door opened. "Electa?" Greer asked. "I never liked that woman. She always came off as a bit snooty. Besides, she sent me a zoning code violation for weeds three weeks ago. Apparently, some vigilant citizen complained. There was one tiny patch of extra growth on the side of the garage."

"Electa sent you the letter?" I would have to double check the letter we received, but I kind of remembered Laverty being the last name of the person who'd signed the citation. "We got a similar letter from the zoning office."

"Electa is a cog in the machine. Nothing more. She started showing up for pop-in inspections when I turned down Clem Hanley's offer to buy the place last year. She works for him at the zoning office."

Parker gawped at his father, then said, "Clem wanted to buy my place as well. I'm not ready to sell, which is what I told him. But that was just two months ago. I just figured he thought I'd put it on the market since I was moving the rescue out of the city limits."

"Theresa had said that Jock and Clem were friends. Jock was godfather to Clem Hanley's son." I shook my head. "I thought the letters were about revenge, but what if they were about property? I'll have to talk to Buzz and Ryan, but I wonder if they got offers on their places as well. You are all zoned for business. But why would Clem want to buy up commercial property in Moonrise?"

And what did it have to do with Jock Simmons?

CHAPTER 14

I'd spent most the night before on my phone searching everything I could find on antifreeze poisoning. There was a disturbing amount of information. I just hoped nobody browsed my search history, or I might become suspect number one. Thank the Goddess I didn't have any homework due today.

I stopped by Buzz and Nadine's house in the morning before class. Nadine's car was in the driveway. I wondered if Buzz's truck had been impounded. Their cute white colonial house with the white picket fence epitomized the small-town American dream. And Buzz had been trying to live the dream with the woman he loved and possibly a child in the future.

His eyes were bloodshot, and the lines in his face deeper than I'd ever seen them. Even though he was in his seventies, by human standards, his appearance was that of a man in his late twenties, early thirties. But today, Buzz could have easily been mistaken for someone in his forties or fifties. Was that because of stress? Or was he physically aging?

"Morning," he grumbled as he welcomed me inside. "Don't you have classes to get to?"

"I have an hour," I told him as we went into the kitchen.

Buzz poured me a cup of coffee. He added two heaping spoons of cream and just as much sugar. "Here you go."

"Thanks. How are you holding up?"

"Crap-tastic," he said.

"Where's Nadine?"

"She's still in bed. We were up late last night talking."

"Is that why you look so tired?"

"And then some." Buzz ran his thumbnail over a scratch in the table. "I don't know if I can last two more months without shifting."

I glanced around, surprised to hear him having this conversation in the house when Nadine was right down the hall.

He grimaced. "She knows."

"What?"

"I told her last night." His knee began to bounce. "I had to. She's been noticing the difference in my mood and behavior. When she confronted me about it last night, I blurted it out."

Trepidation tightened my throat. "How'd that go over?" The answer was important. If Nadine knew what Buzz was, then she also knew I was a shifter as well. Would she hate me for keeping the truth from her? Goddess help me, I knew I was feeling selfish, worrying about how Buzz's revelation would affect my relationship with Nadine, but I couldn't help it. "Is she mad? Frightened? Freaked out?"

"All of the above," he said. "At first she thought I was crazy. She even talked about us visiting a shrink or checking into a clinic. I think, on some level, she was already planning my insanity defense."

"How did you convince her?"

"The same way you convinced Parker." He gave me a flat stare. "I turned my hands furry and showed her my claws."

"Oh, my."

"Yep, that went about as well as you can imagine. It took me almost an hour to talk her out of leaving."

"Damn, Buzz. I'm sorry this is happening to you, but I wished you would have waited to tell her. At least, do it when there wasn't a big crisis."

His brow furrowed. "Don't you think I know that? I'd love to turn back time to the second before I blurted it out and superglue my mouth shut."

"How did you all leave it?"

"She stayed," he said. "I guess that's all I can ask for right now."

"That's something." I took a sip of my coffee. "It took Parker months to come to terms with what we are, but he eventually did. Nadine will come around. She loves you."

"But Parker has your scent, and you have his. You both have a supernatural bond that can help smooth out the rough times. I don't have that with Nadine."

"I think you'd be surprised at the capacity humans have for love, even without a magical nudge."

"I hope you're right. If you're not…" He placed his hands over his face. "I don't even want to think about it."

"Not shifting has gotten you in trouble. You are having a tough time mentally, physically, and emotionally. Maybe you should just shift all the way. At least you'll feel more like yourself. After things settle, you can try again. You know, if you both still want it."

"Not being truthful is what got me in trouble. I should have either told Nadine the truth before we moved in together, or I should have moved on."

"Did she say that?"

He sighed. "No."

"When we clear your name, you and Nadine will have some time to work things out."

"You mean if my name gets cleared."

"No, I mean when. Jock didn't die from the stab wound."

Buzz leaned forward and ran his fingers down the side of his beard. "Really?"

"It was antifreeze poisoning."

"Could it have been accidental?"

"I don't think so. But it means that someone was killing him days before he wound up in your parking lot."

"What's this about antifreeze?" Nadine walked into the kitchen. Her chestnut brown hair was flat on one side and messy on the other, and her pale-green eyes were puffy.

"Hi," I said, unsure of how to talk to my friend now that she knew my biggest secret.

Nadine stared at me as if trying to decide if she wanted to slap me or kick me out. She did neither. "Hey." She got herself a cup of coffee. She and Buzz didn't make eye contact when she sat down. I thought she would have questions for me about Buzz's midnight reveal, and I braced myself for whatever repercussions that were coming my way.

Imagine my surprise when the only thing she said was, "Tell me what you know."

If she didn't want to talk about the werecougars in the room, I wasn't about to push it. "Jock died of poisoning, not the stabbing. The knife or whatever he was stabbed with didn't cut any vital organs or arteries. Nothing he wouldn't have survived. The antifreeze caused kidney failure, and it made his lungs fill with fluid. Essentially, he couldn't breathe and suffocated to death."

Her cheeks colored with interest. "But does antifreeze kill someone immediately?"

"Not usually. He could have been having symptoms for a while."

"So, he was already dying when Buzz punched him?"

Buzz's head jerked up. "Was he?"

I nodded. "He had to have been." I remembered the sweet smell on him and his slurred speech. "I thought he was drunk, but it could have been a side effect of the ethylene glycol."

"How do you know all this?"

I gave her a stare that said, who do you think? But said, "An anonymous source."

"Uh-huh." Nadine wiped a dribble of coffee from her lip. "I see." For a micro-second, the side of her mouth turned up into a half-smile. Just as rapidly, it went away.

"Did you find out about the call? Did the sheriff's station get a report about the break-in at The Cat's Meow?" I asked.

"Sheriff Avery has shut me down completely. He's threatened everyone connected to the case that if they share information with me, he'll put them on suspension."

"He threatened Reggie, too."

Nadine released a huffing sigh. "He's such a dick."

I raised my hand. "Preach."

"I need to get back to work." Buzz stood up and dumped his coffee in the sink. "This is the first time in twelve years that I haven't opened on a Thursday."

"I think your regulars will understand," I said.

"Then you don't understand humans very well."

"Neither do you," Nadine snapped.

Uh-oh. This was about to go down.

"I better get to class," I said.

Nadine pinned me with a stare. "You stay put, Lily Mason."

Yep. Things were about to blow up.

"I don't know what else to say to you," Buzz said. He slammed his cup into the sink. When he turned to face us, his dark-emerald eyes had turned bright green.

I jumped up. "Buzz!" I turned my gaze to Nadine. She had tears in her eyes. "He needs to shift, Nadine. The full moon is Saturday, and he's feeling it hard."

"How is any of this real?" Nadine asked. "I've seen it, but I can't wrap my mind around it. I keep thinking that this is a bad dream, and I'm going to wake up at any minute."

"Is it really so awful?" I asked. "Nothing has changed. I'm still me. Buzz is still Buzz."

She shook her head. "When you're not furry and walking on all fours." She stared at me. "Why didn't you tell me? I tell you everything, Lily. Everything."

I glowered at Buzz. I couldn't throw him under the bus. He was the biggest reason I hadn't told Nadine, but if I told her that, she'd never forgive him. "I regret not telling you, but it's not just my secret to share. There are shifter communities all over the country. Every time we show our truth to a human, we take a chance that we're exposing all of our kind. You've seen enough to know that there are folks who would have us imprisoned, or worse, exterminated."

She appeared heartbroken. "Do you really believe I'd betray you?"

"No."

"You should have told me."

Buzz sat down in the chair next to Nadine. His shoulders slumped in defeat. "This is my fault. I asked Lily not to tell you."

"Why?"

He balled his hands into fists. "Because I was afraid."

"Of what?"

"Of losing you."

"How did you think you were going to keep this from

me?" She turned to me. "How old are you? Buzz said he was seventy-six"

"I'm thirty-seven."

"This blows my mind so hard." She rubbed her cheeks and blew out a harsh breath. "How did you think I wouldn't notice that you weren't aging? It was bound to come up sometime down the road. Or worse, did you just figure on leaving me before any questions came up?" These questions were directed mostly at Buzz.

"Honestly," he said. "I don't know."

"Why did you move in with me? Why did we talk about babies? You made me believe we had a future." She studied me for a moment. "And does Parker know?"

"Yes."

Her expression darkened. "I don't know where to go from here. What am I supposed to do with all this?"

"I hope you'll forgive me and accept me. You're one of my best friends, and I don't know what I'd do without you in my life, but I'd stay away if that's what you wanted."

"I just need some time to think about this."

"How long?" Buzz asked.

"Longer than a minute," she replied. "It's a whole lot. I mean, I see you. Both of you, but it's like finding out your favorite dog is really a cat. You still love it, but it's a shocker."

"What I hear," I said, "is that you still love us?"

She rolled her eyes. "Of course, I love you. I'm not so sure about Mister Cut-and-Run, but you, Lily, yes."

"I love you, Nadine. I love you more than I thought I could love anyone. I would stay for as long as you wanted me."

Nadine fixed him with her gaze. "I'm going to get old and gray, and you aren't."

"I'm not immortal. I'll eventually get old."

"But I'll get older faster." Her lips thinned in a grim frown. "What then?"

"Then I make every moment of our life together count until I can't. And hey, I could always get hit by a bus. It's not like I can't be killed."

"Well, there's always that," she said.

I cleared my throat. "It seems you two have some more talking to do, and I have a class I've got to get to."

CHAPTER 15

O n the way to school, all I could think about, aside from Buzz and Nadine, was the phone call. Buzz had said it came from the police. It should be logged on his phone. Was the sheriff's department looking into it at all? I hated that the sheriff was not even open to the idea that there might be other suspects. And who in the heck was the witness? I still didn't understand what the person could have possibly seen him doing other than trying to stop the bleeding?

My composition class' first lesson was on reading and analyzing text to determine the value of the information. Mr. Danby, a short man with a receding hairline, opened the class with, "The past, the present, and the future walk into a bar. Man, was it tense."

Several of us chuckled uncomfortably.

Then he explained that the joke was funny because

writing involves past tense, present tense, and future tense.

You could hear a pin drop. I felt bad for the guy.

I went to my botany class, hoping it would be another short one. My hope paid off. When I got to the classroom, several students were standing outside the room. A younger student, a guy about the age of twenty, said, "There's a note on the door. Class is canceled today."

"Does it say why?"

He shook his head. "Nope. Just that we're to read chapters one and two then complete the odd questions at the end of each chapter to turn in next Tuesday." Several students groaned. I was just happy to have more time to figure out how to save Buzz.

What was next? I felt as if the investigation had ground to a halt. My next stop was to find out what I could about Clem Hanley and his son James, along with Electa Laverty. They were certainly up to no good, but was their hinky behavior related to Jock's death or merely coincidental? This would all be easier if I had a crystal ball, but not even witches, the real kind, could foresee the future.

As I drove through town, I decided that the purple-pink flowers covering knobby, gnarled redbud trees were my new favorite color. The native tree decorated the streets with its unusual beauty. I'd skimped on breakfast this morning, and with the full moon so close, I was hungrier than normal. The Moonrise Drive-in had recently opened up. It reminded me of a hometown Dairy Queen type place. Basically, fast food and custard ice cream. Yum. And that's all it took to talk me into stopping there for an early lunch.

The gravel parking lot was packed, and I thanked the Goddess my truck was tiny. I squeezed in between a white SUV and an electric-blue four-door sedan. There were two picnic tables in a grassy area occupied by seven elderly men in coveralls and John Deere hats, and several people were sitting on the tails of their trucks, eating burgers and sucking down large fountain drinks and shakes.

The menu was on a board that stretched from one end of the drive-in's exterior wall to the other. I got in line for the order window. My mouth watered at the smell of frying hamburgers and onion rings, but the picture of the giant tenderloin on a bun screamed, eat me!

"I heard he stabbed him five times right in the parking lot," I overheard a woman say.

"I heard he shot him and stabbed him."

I rolled my eyes. People liked to talk. It wasn't a crime, but I wanted to seek them out and smack them into next week. I took a deep breath. This damn full moon was going to get all the Masons in trouble. I danced on my toes and concentrated on the menu. Root beer float, that was a definite yes. Onion rings. Yes, yes. Fried cheese balls. Oh, hellz yes. And they had Pups-cream. A vanilla ice cream cone with a doggy treat on top. Free when you brought your pooch with you. I saw a trip to the drive-in in Smooshie's near future.

I had to stop reading the board. Otherwise, I was going to buy everything. There was a door on the far side of the pick-up window. I assumed it was for employees, but I saw two geriatric women knock on the door, one with snowball white hair and one with hot-pink hair. Unless the Moonrise Drive-in was hiring retirees, Opal and Pearl were not employees. I saw Opal say something right before she went inside. Then Pearl knocked, and I tuned out the crowd so I could hear what she said.

"The crow flies south," she said. The door opened, and she went inside.

There were only three people ahead of me now. A fierce debate between my stomach and my curiosity raged in my head. Did I keep my place and order food? Or did I poke my nose into Opal and Pearl's business?

There was a reason for the saying, curiosity killed the cat.

Dang it all!

With great reluctance, I stepped out of line. I went to the door and knocked.

"Which way does the crow fly?" someone asked on the other side.

"The crow flies south," I replied.

The door opened again. A man in a white hat and grease-stained apron ushered me inside. There was a *"do not enter*" sign on the door behind him. He jerked his thumb toward it. "Ten dollars buys you thirty minutes. Twenty dollars buys you an hour. If you want longer, you must exit and then come back."

Pulling out my wallet hurt, because ten dollars might not seem like a lot of money, but for me, every nickel counted. Still, I had to know what was on the other side of that wall! I hoped it wasn't anything dirty, because I didn't think I could ever use enough mind bleach to scrub the sight of Opal or Pearl doing the sexy. Eek.

Even more reluctantly than I'd given up my place in the food line, I handed over two fives. The guy opened the door. I entered with trepidation, but seeing Opal and Pearl, along with a man in a pair of black pants, a white button-down shirt, and a tie, all sitting down at video poker machines, lessened my anxiety.

"Lily!" Pearl said. "I've not seen you here before. You must do all your gambling at Langdon's."

As in Langdon's One-Stop? I was still confused by what I was seeing. Opal and the man were pushing buttons on the machines as I sat down to the only open one on the other side of Pearl.

"What do I do?"

"Oh, you're a virgin," she said, nudging me with her bony shoulder. She poo-pooed her hand. "I love it. Just put money in that slot and start playing."

"To what purpose?"

"To win money, of course."

"We can win money?"

"You really are a video poker newbie," she cackled. "Watch me."

She hit the button on her machine to bet one dollar on the hand. Five cards came up, a king of hearts, a two of clubs, king of spades, a ten of diamonds, and a two of hearts. She pushed the hold button on the two kings, and the two twos then pressed deal. A two of clubs replaced the ten of diamonds.

"Yes!" she cried out as she won ten dollars on the hand. "I'm a winner, baby!"

"Settle down, Pearl," Opal said.

"You're just mad because you ain't me," she told her sis.

"I had no idea Moonrise had gambling," I said to Pearl.

"I've never been anywhere that didn't have gambling or bookmaking. It doesn't matter where I've lived."

"Is this legal?"

Pearl leaned in conspiratorially. "It's legal unless you get caught."

I knew from Opal that they had lived in Las Vegas for many years. Pearl had been married to an accountant who worked for the mafia. He'd abused her, and Opal killed him for it. I put a dollar in the machine in front of me but eyed the sisters warily. Would they have killed

Jock? I'd watched a Discovery show on murder, and it was mentioned that poison tended to be a woman's weapon.

I couldn't see a clear motive for them. I mean, I think boredom was Pearl's only motivation, and Opal, as I'd learned, would do anything to protect Pearl. But could Pearl have gotten bored enough to murder? I doubted it.

I bet a quarter, the minimum bid, and watched as a three of clubs, four of clubs, king of clubs, eight of diamonds, and a queen of clubs came up on the screen.

"Hold all the clubs," Pearl said.

I did as she said. An ace of spades replaced the eight.

"Shoot." Pearl rapped my knee with her arthritic knuckles. "Keep trying."

"When is Buzz opening the diner?" Opal asked. She didn't glance up from her machine. "I don't want to have to find a new spot to people watch in the afternoons."

"I don't know. Probably tomorrow. He just needed a day." I wasted another quarter on a losing hand.

"Well, tell him we are all rooting for him. I don't believe for a minute he killed Jock Simmons, not because he's not capable, but because he's not stupid enough to get caught in the act," Opal said. "Obviously."

I smiled even as I lost my fourth hand and the last of my dollar. "That's no lie."

"Mike Avery has his head so far up his own butt, he couldn't see obvious if it smacked him in the nuts," Pearl said.

The man in the tie snorted a laugh.

I giggled. "You guys are the most."

"And don't you forget it," Pearl said.

"Well, I've lost my money, so I'm out. Good luck, you all." I could still smell the food, and so after I exited the building, I got back in line. When I made it to the front, finally, I ordered a Bonanza burger, a giant tenderloin, onion rings, fried cheese balls, and a root beer float. When my order was ready, I picked it up at the far window. It was then I noticed a small sign that said, *Trinity Commercial Real Estate, Buy. Sell. Lease. Call 555-289-3434.*

I called the number.

A robo-voice answered: *You've reached Trinity Commercial Real Estate. We buy, sell, and lease commercial property. Please leave your name, phone number, and a brief message about why you are calling, and we will return your call as soon as possible. Beep.*

Straight to voice mail. Interesting.

CHAPTER 16

I called the zoning office when I got back into my truck and asked for Electa Laverty. The person who answered said Electa wouldn't be in to work this week. I took a chance and asked where she was, but I was told that they weren't allowed to give out personal information. After, I drove straight to Buzz's house. I wanted to see how he was doing, but also, I hoped Nadine would still be home. I hauled the food and the float up the stoop with me.

Buzz answered the door. He frowned. "Did you bring enough for everyone?"

"What do you think?"

"I think I'm making my own lunch," he said.

"You're such a smart man," I told him. "If you're nice, I'll share my onion rings."

He made a face. "What are you doing back?"

"I was hoping to catch Nadine."

"She's showering. She's on patrol tonight."

I put the bags of food on the glass coffee table in the living room. I heard the shower running, so I asked, "How are things between the two of you?"

"Strained, but not over." He shook his head. "I'll take it. I can get through anything as long as she doesn't leave me."

"I know it's rotten timing, but I'm glad you were honest with her. I really wish I could have been here, though. It's hard knowing that two people you love have been lying to you from the get-go. I hope she can forgive us."

"Me too," he said. I heard the shower shut off. Shortly, Nadine strode down the hallway with her hair and body wrapped in towels. "Buzz, do you know where my round brush is?" She saw me and blinked. "Lily, what are you doing here?"

"Did you know the new Moonrise Drive-in has gaming machines in a back room?" I spoke hurriedly as if Nadine might kick me out before I could finish. "You have to give a password phrase and everything to get inside. I paid ten bucks to play for twenty minutes. That's shady, right? And I think Langdon's One-Stop has the same setup."

"We've heard about the gambling in town," she said, sitting on the arm of the brown microfiber couch. "But the sheriff never wants to investigate."

"He doesn't, huh?" I scratched my head as my conversation with Greer about Hanley ran through my head. "Did Clem Hanley offer to buy The Cat's Meow, Buzz?"

"About six months ago," he said. "He offered a fair price, but I don't plan to give up my place in Moonrise." He gave Nadine a meaningful look.

"He made an offer to Parker and Greer, as well," I told him.

"What does this have to do with gambling?" she asked.

"Nothing or everything," I said. "It could be a coincidence, but there's a Trinity Commercial Real Estate company listed as the owner of the property leased by the Moonrise Drive-in. I wonder if Clem has been buying up property to sell to them?"

Nadine scooted far enough forward that her upper thigh was exposed. Buzz, with the familiarity of long-term coupling, pulled it down for her. She frowned up at him, her expression a mixture of longing and confusion. I think it was the first time they'd touched since Buzz's revelation.

Nadine's gaze flitted to me. "That time when the bar was on fire, and you pulled me to safety. Did you do it in your cougar form?"

All I could do was tell the truth. "Yes. I couldn't get you out fast enough in my human body, so I changed."

"All this time." She shook her head and laughed once. "I

thought the smoke had made me delirious. It's hard to be mad at someone who saved your life."

"It's hard having you mad at me. You're my first and best friend in this town. I don't want to lose that."

"Your round brush is in the third drawer on the right with your curl lotion," Buzz said.

"You always know," Nadine told him. She got up to go back to the bathroom. Before she left the living room, she said, "I'll check into the gambling and Hanley and see what I can find out."

"You're the best," I said.

She grinned. "Yes, I am."

I FINISHED LUNCH AT BUZZ'S THEN DROVE OUT TO PETRY'S Pet Clinic to work my Thursday afternoon shift. I'd missed my hours the previous morning so I couldn't miss any more time this week. Unfortunately, I would barely have enough money to cover my bills this month, but, over the years, I'd managed to turn living paycheck to paycheck into an art form.

Where the shelter smelled strongly of dogs, no matter how much we cleaned, the clinic held a countless number of odors. I found it difficult in my human form to distinguish one from another. On top all of the animal scents, there was a distinct aroma of medicine, disinfectant, and kibble.

"Afternoon, Lily," Abby Levine, a petite black woman, and the head receptionist, greeted me. She wore her chin-length hair straight and cut asymmetrically, and it complimented her angular face. Abby was the kind of woman who always seemed put together.

There were two men—one with a beagle on a leash, the other holding a Pomeranian in his arms—and a young woman with an adorable white kitten in a carrier waiting for their appointments.

"Hi, Abby." I strolled past the reception desk to the examination area just on the other side. I took a spur-of-the-moment detour into the kennel area to check on Hester. Ryan had told Parker he wanted to observe her for a few days, but even though he expected her to fully recover, I wanted to check on her myself. The large brindle was lying on a cot covered in clean blankets.

"Hey, sweetheart," I said as I unlatched the gate. She was slow to get up, but her eyes appeared clear, her tail wagged, and she had the best smile on her face when I got down on my knees to greet her. Hester had had her ears cropped when she was young, which could make pit bulls seem intimidating, but there was nothing about this seventy-five-pound bundle that wasn't love. She'd been overbred eight times in a puppy mill, and when she was too old to have more babies, she'd been abandoned at a dump. To see the dog she was now, to the dog she'd been when we'd taken her in three months ago, was amazing. "How are you feeling, girlfriend?"

She licked my face.

"Better, huh? I bet you're ready to go back to a cozy house." I booped her nose. "No more drinking bad stuff," I told her. "I'll check on you again before I go." I gave her a good scratching behind the ears and on her butt before leaving the large kennel.

I went back to the exam area and peeked around the corner of the workspace, where Ryan kept medications, lab specimens, a refrigerator, and diagnostic equipment. It was an area strictly off-limits to non-employees.

Ryan hovered over a microscope, studying a slide.

I crept up behind him and goosed his side.

"Ah!" He jerked to attention and hit the top of his scalp against the cabinet directly above the counter. "Ow, crap." His hand went to the top of his head.

I was simultaneously appalled and amused. I threw my hand over my mouth to cover my laugh. "I'm so sorry! My bad."

He grimaced as he rubbed his head. "Your apology would sound more sincere if you weren't giggling."

I reached up and touched the newly formed bump on his crown.

"Ouch," he said.

"Dang, you whacked it hard. I'll get you some ice." I took a cold pack from the fridge and handed it to him. "Don't fire me."

Even in pain, he flashed me his signature flirty smile. "I'll fire you next week." He leaned back against the counter, still holding the ice pack to his injury. "How are you doing? I can't believe it about Jock. And they arrested Buzz. How crazy is that?"

"Pretty crazy." For the first time since Buzz had shown up at my trailer, it all hit me.

Ryan put down the ice pack. He fast-grabbed some tissues out of a box on the counter and thrust them at me. "Don't cry, Lily."

I sniffled and dabbed my eyes. "I'm not." The tears and snot were telling a different story. I blew my nose. "I'm fine. Fine."

He gave me an *uh-huh, right* look. The only thing missing between the arched brow and pursed lips was the head bob. "I can tell," he said flatly.

"Buzz is innocent," I told him. "He didn't kill Jock."

"Lily," Ryan said, his voice gentle. "Of course Buzz didn't do it." He put his arm over my shoulder. "How can I help you?"

I glanced up at him. "You just did." I clapped my hands and stepped away from him. "Now, give me something to do, boss man."

"Help Kelly with the next patient exam. It's an itty-bitty kitty." He chucked my chin with a crooked index finger. "Kittens make everything better."

"Yay. They really do."

Kelly, one of Ryan's VTAs, or veterinarian technician assistant, the job I was angling for, popped her head around the corner. While we were both redheads, my coloring was more cinnamon while hers was a lighter ginger. She smiled at me. "Lily, do you want to bring back Ms. Jackson with her new baby, Pillow?"

"Oh my gosh, the kitten's name is Pillow? I can't stand it." The cuteness overwhelmed! "I'll bring him... Her?"

"Him," Kelly said.

"Even more adorable. I'll bring them back." I strode through the exam area to reception.

Our volunteer Jordan walked through the front door. When she saw me, she looked astonished. "Lily, I forgot you work here on Thursdays." A slight, yet sharp aroma of vinegar hit my nose, even over all the other scents in the reception area.

"Hi, Jordan. What are you up to today?" She wasn't on the volunteer schedule at the shelter today, and I knew she wasn't taking summer classes.

"I wanted to check on Hester. Keith told me yesterday that Hester had been taken to the vet, and I was on this side of town, so I thought I'd stop in and check on her."

Jordan had started volunteering the month before the Blakes took Hester in as a foster. I loved the bonds that our team formed with the pit bulls, even the ones we only had for a short while. "That's so sweet of you to check on her. I'll ask Ryan if you can go back and see her. Do you have time to wait a few minutes?" Plus, I'd wanted to talk to her about James Hanley, and this was the perfect opportunity.

"Absolutely," she said.

"Just let me take Ms. Jackson and Pillow back."

The basic exam of the kitten included weighing him, taking his temperature, and observing for any physical abnormalities. After Kelly and I determined the cute-as-hell fluff ball appeared to be perfect, Ryan came in and charmed the pants off Ms. Jackson as he did a head-to-toe assessment of the kitten, checking his teeth, eyes, nose, ears, and genitals. Well, the lack of genitals. Kittens as young as Fluffy didn't have prominent privates.

The kitten flopping on its back and playfully batted at Ryan's hands with his tiny toe beans. His cuteness melted me into a puddle. "He's such an adorable baby," I told Ms. Jackson.

She grinned hard enough to make *my* cheeks hurt.

Ryan nodded his agreement. "Congratulations, Ms. Jackson. Pillow is a healthy one-pound two-ounce six-week-old cutie-patootie. Did Abby go over the kitten package with you?"

"She sure did," Ms. Jackson said.

"Great. So today, we'll get his initial vaccinations done, and we'll see you in two weeks for the next ones. Did you bring in a stool sample?"

Ms. Jackson proudly held out a plastic baggy with a tiny poop ribbon inside. "I got it right before we came here."

"Perfect," Ryan said, hitting her with a devastating smile.

I heard her heartbeat kick up a notch. Ryan was gay, but not many people in town knew. Still, it didn't stop him from flirting with anything on two legs. I loved that about him. "I'll go check for heartworms while Kelly and Lily get the vaccinations done. Okay?"

"Just fine, Doctor Ryan. Thank you." I half expected the woman to start fanning herself.

Kelly and I grinned at each other as we followed Ryan into the workspace. Kelly retrieved a vial of DHLPP vaccine, which protected cats from distemper, hepatitis, leptospirosis, parainfluenza, and the parvovirus. We would give the cat a dewormer as well if the stool specimen showed any critters. While she was logging the lot number, I went over to Ryan, who was preparing a poop slide.

"Jordan Deeter, one of the volunteers from the rescue is here."

"I remember Jordan," he said, frowning in deep concentration as he finished the prep and was moving the slide under the microscope for examination. "Does she need something?"

"She wants to check on Hester, if that's okay."

"Without a doubt. If you want, why don't you take Hester out for some activity? It'll be good for her to stretch her legs. Her hips are a little arthritic, so lying down for long periods of time can make her stiff."

I'd noticed that when she'd gotten up from the cot. "Thanks. I'll do that right after we get done with the vaccine."

"Go on," Kelly said. "Pillow is pretty calm. I think between Ms. Jackson and me, we should be able to get one injection done. You'll do Hester a lot of good."

"Can I just say how much I love working here?"

Ryan chuckled. "You just did."

"We love having you, Lily. The animals, no matter how sick or feisty, seem to really calm down when you're here. I'm going to start asking Ryan to call you in for all the hard cases," Kelly said.

"If I'm not at the shelter, you can have me," I said, grateful to have found my way to Moonrise, Missouri.

CHAPTER 17

This morning, the meteorologist on channel five had called for showers on Friday and thunderstorms on Saturday, but today was just gorgeous outside. The sun was shining, there was a slight breeze, and it was a perfect seventy-two degrees. Jordan and I watched Hester trot around the big fenced-in area until she began to circle.

"Poop patrol," Jordan said.

We both laughed. "They love to circle before they come in for a landing."

"They really do." She laughed again. "I was really worried about her when I found out she got sick."

"Me too. She's such a sweet old girl. I don't understand people who go out of their way to hurt animals. There has to be something wrong inside them. Deeply wrong."

"Yes," Jordan agreed. "It's terrible." I heard such heartbreak in her voice that I reached out to touch her. Jordan reflexively stepped away before my fingers made contact with her.

I'm a shifter, and touch is vital to my kind. Hugs, holding hands, a hand on the shoulder, arm, or knee, is all about showing love, support, and comfort, and I'd been lucky to find friends and family here in Moonrise who equally craved, or at least enjoyed, physical contact. However, I'd learned to respect someone's preferences when they made it clear they weren't comfortable being touched. So, I let my hand drop.

"How are classes going?"

"Good. A sculpture of mine was chosen to be displayed at the Two Hills Museum of Modern Art on campus for the summer."

"That's great," I told her. "Congratulations. I'll stop in and take a gander next week after classes." When she didn't say more, I decided to broach the subject of James. I started with subtle. "Are you seeing anyone?"

She shook her head. "Not anymore."

Not a lie. Hmm. "I saw you with James Hanley at the courthouse the other morning. I thought you two—"

Jordan shook her head. "It isn't like that. I grew up with James. My parents and his used to be friends."

"Used to?"

She gave a startled blink. "I mean, they're friends."

My internal lie detector pinged hard, which seemed weird for such a small lie. "What do your parents do?"

"They used to own a florist shop here in town." Truth.

"Are they retired? Do they travel?" I always thought I'd want to travel someday. Maybe, after my degree, I could start saving money for a trip with Parker.

Jordan shook her head. "Not yet. Maybe after I finish up college."

Truth. "Do you know Addy Newton?"

"Sure. Why?"

"He's home for the summer. He'll be taking on some volunteer hours several days a week until the fall semester starts back up."

"Wow. That'll be great when we open up the new center." She whistled for Hester, and the brindle baby trotted over. "Such a good girl," Jordan said, cupping Hester's jowls and giving them a playful squeeze. "Do we have everything we need for the opening?" She picked up a ball on the grass and tossed it. Hester took off after it.

"Just about," I said. Hester barked and rolled as she dived for the ball. I laughed. "We're lucky to have so many talented volunteers. Your murals are fantastic."

"Thank you, Lily. It's some of my favorite work."

We'd moved on from James, the Hanleys, and her parents. Well played, Jordan, well played. But I wouldn't be deterred. "Aren't James and Addy younger than you?"

"I graduated two years before them."

"Addy says he saw James' truck at the shelter on Monday night."

"I wouldn't let someone who isn't an official volunteer into the shelter at night." Honestly, she looked really upset. "I swear it. I talked to him in the parking lot for about ten minutes, but he didn't stay, and I certainly didn't let him in."

Shoot. Truth. "I didn't mean to imply you would."

"I have to go."

Ping.

Jordan knelt next to Hester and gave her one last cuddle. "Thanks for getting me access to Hester. I'm so relieved to see her doing so well."

"The shelter is lucky to have someone like you looking out for our pretty pooches."

She nodded. "See you soon."

I played with Hester for another fifteen minutes before taking her back inside. I couldn't help feeling unsettled by my talk with Jordan. I believed her about James, but there was something she was holding back. The problem was, did the secret have to do with Jock's death? Or was it truly none of my business?

AFTER MY SHIFT, I DROVE STRAIGHT TO PARKER'S HOUSE. I couldn't stop thinking about Nadine and Buzz, and everything that Buzz had risked trying to have a baby, then him nearly blowing up their relationship with his truth bomb. On top of that, I was certain that Clem Hanley was somehow neck deep in whatever bull crap Jock was into, but I couldn't manage to connect any dots. There was gambling and offers to buy out businesses, and zoning violations being sent left and right. And what of the elusive Electa Laverty? I wanted to talk to the woman, but if I found her, what in the world could I say? It wasn't like I had any ties to her, no friends or work in common. But if she had been Jock's current lover, she might have a good idea who would want to kill him and why. Also, she might be the killer herself. I mean, if Jock was my guy, he would have been dead long before now.

This mystery had pieces from several different puzzles all thrown into the same box. It felt as if no matter how many times I tried to put it together, the picture was never going to make any sense.

When I let myself into Parker's house, I sat down on the floor in the living room and asked, "Can I get a hug?" Smooshie, who had barreled in from the kitchen, obliged me by hitting me with a running tackle followed by wet, aggressive kisses. I laughed, rolling on the carpet as she bounced around me.

"While the men are away the girls will play," Parker said when he brought Elvis in from the backyard.

"Party over here," I said, sitting up. Smooshie plopped her booty right onto my lap.

"You two are something else," Parker said.

"Too much?" I asked.

"Never." He gave me a hand up and kissed me hard. "So, tell me what's going on?"

"You mean other than Buzz being arrested for murder, and I'm not any closer to the truth than I was two days ago?"

"No, I mean, whatever new thing has got you feeling vulnerable."

I stared at him for a moment. "How do you do that?"

"Do what?"

"You know me so well."

"That's because you've let me. You've told me everything about your life. You've been so honest, that it's let me be just as honest. When two people hide nothing from each other, reading emotional cues is easy."

When he used words like emotional cues, I knew he was

channeling his PTSD counselor. "Did you go see your shrink this morning?"

Parker chuckled, and the sound stirred up a longing in me. "Yes." He tapped my nose. "See, you know me well, too."

Except, I was keeping something from him. Something big, and I wasn't sure how to bring it up.

"Just tell me, Lily. I can see you are bothered. Whatever it is, we will work through it together." He cupped my face, and I arose on my tiptoes and met his mouth as he dipped his head to kiss me. "Now, what is it?"

"You know how I told you about Buzz not shifting so he could have a baby with Nadine."

Parker's expression darkened, but he nodded his head. "Yes."

"Buzz told Nadine the truth about him. About us. He blurted it out last night apparently during a fight."

Parker groaned. "He didn't."

I nodded. "I went over there this morning with no idea what I was walking into."

Parker pulled me in for a tight hug. "I'm sorry. How is Nadine? Is she mad at you? Is this why you're so tense?"

"It's part of it," I admitted. "I think she'll come around, but she's hurt we weren't honest with her."

"I'll admit it was a shock for me," he said, "and we weren't even dating at the time."

I tilted my head back. "But you loved me despite our differences."

"I hope you don't think that. I love you because you're you. Every side of you."

"What about children?" I blurted. "Do you want kids?"

Parker grew quiet, his eyes had a far off look in them. "Honestly?"

"Of course." My heart sped up as I waited for his response.

"Lily. Elvis, Smooshie, and all the dogs we rescue, those are the only kids I want. I know there's a chance you can have a baby, now with what Buzz has learned, and I'll consider it if that's what you really want."

A sob escaped me.

"I'm sorry, babe. Really. I'm not trying to hurt you. When you told me it would be impossible for us to have children because I'm human, I just assumed we'd never have this conversation."

I met his gaze, his face blurred through my tears. "I don't want any children. I never have. I had to raise my brother when I was seventeen, and he was seven, and then I had to outlive him. I don't want to do that again. Ever. I can't tell you how relieved I am that you feel the same way."

I wiped my eyes with the back of my hand. Parker had the biggest smile on his face. "You're amazing."

"I'm a pibble mom." I looked over to the couch where Smooshie and Elvis had cuddled up. "Of course I'm amazing."

"Why don't you invite Buzz and Nadine over for dinner tomorrow night? It's a Friday. I can make tacos or lasagna."

"Lasagna," I said. "And let's make three of them."

"So, that's a yes to dinner?"

"Yes. As long as Nadine doesn't have to work."

"And then I can answer the big question. How do you love a Shifter?"

"What's the answer?"

"The exact same way you loved them before you knew." His blue eyes sparkled.

"Good answer."

"So, who do you think killed Jock?"

I jutted my lip in a pout. "I don't know. He was poisoned, which could mean the killer is a woman. But he was also stabbed, but only once. I mean, if you want to kill a guy with a knife, wouldn't you stab, stab, stab?"

Parker nodded. "I'd probably use a garrote. You can't

beat strangling for the personal touch. However, if it was business, I might use a long-range weapon."

"You've given this way too much thought."

"Believe me. As much as I haven't murdered anyone, there are a few people who get to take part in the fantasy."

"Back in my hometown of Paradise Falls, there are several people I've wanted to put my hands on, so I understand."

"I know you have a list of suspects, so let's hear them." He nodded toward the kitchen. "In there, so I can make you something to eat. Your stomach is doing an angry dance against me."

As if to emphasize, a rushing gurgling noise emanated from my tummy. "Tacos?" I asked.

"It's because I mentioned them earlier, right?"

I nodded enthusiastically. "Yep."

He opened the fridge and took out a three-pound package of hamburger while I admired the view. "What have you put together so far?" he asked.

"Is it legal to be on the zoning commission and own a realty company? It just seems really unethical."

"Unethical, definitely. Illegal, probably not. The town council makes the rules, and most of them are old buddies."

"I wish I knew where to start with tracking down Electa

Laverty. Pearl Dixon says they were lovers, she's the inspection officer who signed all the citations, and Jock hasn't...hadn't," I amended, "been spending any time at his own house, but he had to be sleeping somewhere."

"So, she killed him?"

"Maybe. I'd have a better sense of her if I could actually talk to her, but I have absolutely no idea where to find her. And, I'm pissed at the police for not bothering to investigate beyond Buzz. He has no real motive. One small fight shouldn't make him the prime suspect, and if Sheriff Avery wasn't controlling the investigation, I think they would already be tracking down other leads."

My phone rang from the other room. I'd left it in my bag. "Shoot. Give me a second." By the time I retrieved it, I'd had one missed call from Nadine. A text message popped up that said, *Call. Urgent.*

"Who is it?" Parker asked.

I held up the phone, so he could see the screen then swiped her name in my contacts to call her back. She picked up on the first ring.

"Hey, I have some information," Nadine said.

"Hold on. Parker's here. I'm going to put you on speaker." I tapped the speaker button and placed the phone on the table. "Go ahead."

"I got ahold of the records for Buzz's phone. He had a call that showed it came from the sheriff's department, but according to our records, we didn't receive a call about a burglary, and we have no calls going out to Buzz's phone."

"Then Buzz can prove that someone sent him over there. Someone pretending to be from the police."

"All it proves is that he got a call. But the prosecution will say that there is no way to say who made the call or what was said, so Buzz's testimony about it is hearsay."

"What about the call that sent you all over to The Cat's Meow at the same time?"

"The call came from an anonymous tip, and the number used traces back to the coin-operated laundry mat here in town. When the logs were pulled for the place, there was no record of a call being made from their phone."

"How is that even possible?"

"I called a forensic scientist we've used in the past for help on cases where we've had to get information from smartphones or computers. He said there are apps that can be downloaded to allow the caller to spoof other numbers."

"Isn't that illegal?"

"Nope," Nadine said. "As long as the call placed is not for malicious intent, the app is perfectly legal to use to hide your real phone number."

"Can it be traced?"

"It depends on how clever the person using the app is. Most of the time, the answer is no, according to my contact." She'd started out the conversation excited, but now she sounded defeated. "The sheriff doesn't see this as enough evidence to drop the charges."

"How did you manage to get the information? I thought he put a cone of silence around you."

"He did, but I have a lot of friends at the department. They weren't going to keep me out of the loop."

"Did you get to hear the recording of the anonymous tip? Could it be the same person that called Buzz?"

"I did," she said. "I digitally recorded it on my phone and stopped by the house. The caller is female. Buzz's caller was male."

"Maybe if he or she used an app to spoof the phone numbers, he or she could have used an app to change the voice," Parker said.

"Yes," I said. "It still might be the same person. It could be our real killer."

"Maybe," Nadine said. "All I know is that if we don't find more evidence to clear Buzz, Sheriff Avery is going to make sure he goes down for this."

I smacked the table. "Why won't he even consider someone else? It's like he strives for incompetence."

"I'm hoping we can vote him out in the next election, but until then, he's the boss."

"What about the gambling? And Trinity Commercial Real Estate?"

"I'm still looking into that. A friend of mine in the records department said she would go through and look for open and closed cases regarding illegal gambling in Moonrise."

"I have a friend at the county clerk's office who might be able to look up the business license for the real estate company. At the very least, it might give us the owners."

"Who?" Nadine asked.

"Keith Porter's mom," I told her. "Apparently the woman lives for some drama."

"There's no better cure for boredom," Nadine said.

We both laughed until she suddenly stopped, as if remembering she was still mad at me. "I'll let you know if I find anything else out."

My heart sank low. I wasn't ready to end the call. "What about Electa Laverty? Can you look up her address for me? Or maybe you could go and talk to her."

"That's right," Nadine said. "Pearl Dixon had said she was having a fling with Jock. What did she call it exactly? I was pretty stressed when she was talking."

"The nasty flamingo," I said.

Nadine snorted. "That's it. I'll see what I can do."

"Before you go," Parker said. "If you're off work tomorrow night, why don't you and Buzz come over for dinner? It sounds like you and I might have a lot in common. And it might make you feel better to, I don't know, talk about it with someone who's gone through it already."

The silence on Nadine's end was painful. I watched the seconds count away on my phone as we waited, breath held, for her to answer.

"Okay," she finally said, then hung up.

I looked at Parker. "Yay. Progress."

Parker smirked. "The nasty flamingo?"

I made a circle with the left thumb and fingers then poked at it suggestively with my right index finger. Parkers eyebrows rose, then he laughed.

Six-ten the next morning, Nadine called me. It was still dark outside, and I'd just come back inside the house from taking Smooshie out for her morning constitution.

"Are you up?" she asked.

"I am," I told her. "Smooshie's bladder waits for no sun. What's up?"

"I got Laverty's address from the mobile data terminal in my cruiser last night. I can swing by, and we could go out to her place and see if she's home."

Smooshie barked excitedly. "How about if I pick *you* up?

Smooshie is anxious for an adventure, and I don't want to ruin your fancy car."

"Deal," she said. Almost hesitantly, she added, "I miss Smooshie."

I smiled. "I miss you too."

CHAPTER 18

Smooshie sat between Nadine and me, but she kept climbing on Nadine's lap to look out the window.

"My gosh, she's a big girl."

"Body shamer," I teased.

Nadine smacked my arm, and I giggled. She gave Smooshie a hug around her neck. "Don't listen to her. You know I adore you and all your magnificent curves."

"What do you know about Electa? Other than her and Jock doing the nasty flamingo."

Nadine groaned. "Gross."

"You're telling me. I never understood why so many women were attracted to him."

"Because he had money," Nadine said. "Wealth has a way of making even the ugliest of souls attractive for some people."

"How are we playing this?" I asked.

"We knock on her door. I'll act official, and you do what you do that gets people talking."

I hadn't told her about my witchy-juice, but maybe my uncle had. "Did Buzz tell you about my ability to know when people are lying?"

"That's not a thing," she said.

"Neither was Shifters until you found out they were."

She grimaced. "Fair point." She gave me a calculated stare. "You know when someone is telling a lie?"

"Yep. Most people. I can't read Parker, but he's an open book for the most part. Everyone else, though...it's like a bell in my head when someone's lying to me."

"So, if I said I lost my virginity when I was sixteen in the back of a Volkswagen..."

Ping. "Lie."

Her eyes widened. "Fine, I was seventeen, and it was in his dingy basement."

Ping. "Lie."

She blinked. "Okay, I was fifteen, and it was in my childhood treehouse."

"Truth," I said. "Seriously, in a treehouse?"

She snickered. "The floor broke while we were doing it and my butt fell through."

I laughed. "I would have totally hung out with you in high school."

"Same," she said fondly. "So, can you do anything else."

"Besides going all fur and fangs? Well, the same magic that helps me spot lies, also makes people spill their secrets to me. Not all the time, but if it's something weighing on them that they want to get off their chests, or minor secrets that they don't really care if someone finds out, they'll tell me."

"After knowing you now for almost two years, a lot of stuff is starting to make sense now. I mean, I couldn't believe how many times I wanted to tell you everything."

I nodded. "Even about Buzz and you doing the nasty flamingo," I said. "Ew."

Nadine grinned. "He's really good at the nasty flamingo, though."

"Yuck!" I laughed and almost missed my turn down Oak Street. "Hold on." I took the corner sharp but managed to make it. Thankfully, it was still early enough that there weren't any other cars on the road. Smooshie rotated in the seat and licked my ear. "Not the ear, girl!"

"You know, your abilities would make you a damn good police officer. Have you ever considered joining the force?"

"I don't want to chase criminals."

"Says the lady who has solved five murders and a bank robbery in the span of eighteen months. And, also, the lady who is chasing down a suspect as we speak."

"*Touché*." This section of town had a lot of old Victorian, Colonial, and Queen Anne homes. "Which one is hers?"

There," Nadine said, pointing at a light-blue Queen Anne style home. "That's Laverty's place." It was an elaborate three-story, beautifully restored nod to the town's history. Not as expensive as Jock's house, but it still ranked high on the "places I'll never be able to afford" list. We parked on the side of the road in front of the house. The sunrise made the entire neighborhood look as if it were being seen through a sepia filter.

"It's pretty," I said. I rolled the windows down about four inches for Smooshie. It was still cool-ish outside so she would be fine in the car for a minute. "If you're good," I told her, "I'll take you to get Pups-cream at the Moonrise Drive-in." Her tail made a loud thunking noise as it slammed into the dashboard. I grinned. "Who am I kidding? I'll take you no matter what. Still," I added. "Behave."

Nadine waited halfway up the concrete walkway for me, and together, we approached the door. "Let's see how badly Electa Laverty wants to unburden," Nadine said, then knocked.

I attuned my ears toward the house. "I hear someone moving around inside."

We waited a few seconds, then Nadine knocked again.

I heard a faint, "Go away."

"She's in there," I said. "She's just not answering the door."

"Ms. Laverty," Nadine said. "I'm Deputy Nadine Booth with the sheriff's department. I have a few questions I want to ask you about Jock Simmons."

"I don't have anything to say!" she yelled.

I heard her footfalls getting farther away, then the hiss of a sliding glass door. "I think she's trying to go out the back."

"You've got to be kidding me," Nadine muttered. "Don't run, Ms. Laverty! You will only make it worse for yourself."

I'm going around back." I raced to the backyard in time to see Electa in a pink housecoat and slippers, trying to pull herself up over a seven-foot privacy fence, and not making any real progress. Nadine was right on my heels.

"What is she doing?"

"Failing," I said as we walked the rest of the way to where Electa had collapsed to cry.

"Leave me alone," she said.

"You're not in trouble," I said with a soothing tone. "We just want to talk."

"I don't want to talk to you." Her face was puffy and red, no makeup, her blonde hair was oily, and she wore the scent of someone who hadn't showered in days. Also, she reeked of booze. "Ms. Laverty. Electa." I held out my hand and pushed all my will toward her. "Why don't you let us help you?"

She stared at me, her expression bleak, then nodded. "Okay." She took my hand, and I pulled her to her feet. "Let's go inside."

Electa's house matched her appearance, messy and smelly. There was an open bottle of vodka on the kitchen counter, a sink full of crusty dishes, food left out on a table, including two open bags of chips, some dip that had gone from creamy to drippy, and a cheese wheel that had a big chunk sliced out of it. It resembled the cheese wheel in Jock's fridge.

"Did you and Jock buy the cheese together?"

Electa looked at me like I'd grown an extra nose. "How did you know?"

"I saw an identical wheel at his house."

Her back stiffened. "Why were you at his house?"

"I was helping his wife, Theresa, to pack a few things."

"That witch!" Electa slapped a bag of chips off the table, and they sprayed all over the floor.

"Settle down," Nadine said. "When was the last time you saw Jock Simmons?"

Electa sighed, her shoulders slumping before she laid her cheek onto the table. "I saw him Sunday."

"You were with him on Sunday?" I asked.

She twisted her head to look at me, then sat up. A chip clung to her cheek. "I saw him," she said sourly. "I wasn't with him."

"Where did you see him?"

Her face went blotchy. "With someone else." She smashed the other bag of chips with an open palm.

"Here, now," Nadine chided. She glanced at me. "Is there any part of your ability that can stop her from being so destructive?"

I shook my head. "'Fraid not."

"Fine," Nadine said. "Who was he with?"

When Electa didn't answer her, I asked her the question. "Electa, who? Who was Jock with?"

"He promised his tomcat days were over, but I caught him kissing another woman!"

"Do you know who?"

She heaved a sob. "No. I was driving home from church when I saw them, and by the time I got turned around, they were gone. I called him, but he hung up on me." Her eyes narrowed into slits as rage filled her voice. "Me!" She thumped her chest. "After all, I've done for him."

I sat down in the chair next to her and put my hand on her forearm. "What have you done for him, Electa?"

Her mouth dropped open a little then closed. She pursed her lips. "I shouldn't say."

"But you want to tell me, don't you?"

The despondent woman nodded. "I do."

"What did you do for him?" I asked again.

"I…I created situations during some of my inspections to fine people he asked me to."

"Like the Moonrise Pit Bull Rescue?"

Her cheeks quivered. "Uh-huh. That bastard! I thought he loved me. I believed him."

"Did you kill him?"

She sat up straight then and stared me straight in the eyes. "No. Didn't that guy who owns the diner do it?"

"No, he didn't," Nadine said with vehemence. "Tell the truth. You killed Jock and pinned it on Buzz."

"No," Electa said. "I would never hurt Jock. Never!"

I looked up at Nadine. "She's telling the truth."

"Your mojo-thingy is wrong," Nadine said. "It has to be."

"It's not. She's being truthful."

Nadine kicked the empty chip bag on the floor. "Damn it!"

I understood her frustration, but I couldn't let an innocent woman—well, at least innocent of murder—go to jail for a crime she didn't commit."

"How long have you been padding inspections with violations?" Nadine asked.

"Two years," Electa said. "Not for Jock, though."

"Then for who?" I asked.

"Clem Hanley," she said. "My boss. He's been skimming money from the extra fines for a long while."

"I have to call the sheriff," Nadine said.

"No." Electa shook her head. "He knows. He already knows about Clem."

"The sheriff is in on the scheme?"

"I threatened to go to the police once, and Clem told me that he had the sheriff in his pocket."

Nadine goggled at me.

"She's not lying." I fought the nausea welling inside me and worked to slow down my rapidly beating heart. Nadine looked just as ill. "What do we do?" I asked. "If Sheriff Avery is corrupt, what chance do we have getting any kind of fair shake for Buzz?"

"We call Bobby," she said. "He's the only one I trust at the department right now."

"He gave you the information about the phone."

She nodded.

"Okay. We take this information to Bobby."

"I won't testify," Electa said. "If you try to make me, I'll say you are lying."

Nadine smirked and pulled her cell phone from her pocket. "I have a recording," she said. "I'll use it if I have to."

Electa moaned. "Go away. Just go."

I got up, and Nadine followed me out the front door. I looked at my truck. Smooshie sat behind the steering wheel, looking, for anyone passing by, like she was ready to go driving. I looked at Nadine. "That was smart. Recording her. I wish I'd have thought of it."

"Me too," she quipped.

"Huh?"

She took her phone from her pocket and pulled up her recorded file folder. It had one file. She pressed play, and it was Buzz's voice telling her he loved her and to have a day as beautiful as she was.

"You were bluffing? I didn't feel the lie."

"That's because I only said I had a recording. I didn't say what the recording contained, so it wasn't a lie. Buzz left it for me on my phone on our anniversary back in January. I play it when I'm feeling low."

"You are formidable, Nadine Booth."

"And don't you forget it." She gestured to Smooshie. "We owe our chauffeur a Pups-cream cone. I'll call Bobby and see if he can meet us at the Moonrise Drive-in."

CHAPTER 19

I'd let Smooshie poop and pee in a small area of grass near the Moonrise Drive-in before I clipped her leash to an eyehole attached to my truck bed, near the back window. She had enough leash that if she jumped over the side, she wouldn't hang herself, and she could sit up on the tail-bed with Nadine and myself if she wanted. She'd gobbled up her Pups-cream cone and amused herself by people watching, which shortly turned into a more interactive game than a spectator sport.

I had flyers for the shelter's open house in my glove box that I gave to anyone who wanted to smoosh them some Smooshie. Nearly twenty people, men, women, and children, came over, asking if they could pet her. She smiled, posed for cute selfies, wiggled her butt, and in general, was a great ambassador for the pit bull breed and the rescue.

I'd talked to one young man for nearly ten minutes on all

the wonderful ways Smooshie improves my life. Before he walked away, he said, "I'll see you at the open house."

"Yes," I said to Nadine. "Maybe, he'll adopt."

"Or maybe he'll ask you out on a date."

"What are you talking about?"

"That guy was hitting on you so hard, Lils. How can you be so good at reading people and so bad all at the same time?" I looked over at the guy, and he winked. I glanced away. Nadine giggled. "Parker better watch out."

"Parker has nothing to worry about. I'm a one-man woman."

Nadine giggled again. "You're a cougar," she said in a quiet voice.

"Yes," I said. "Why is that funny?"

"No." She smirked. "You're over a decade older than Parker. You are not only a literal cougar, you're also a cougar, cougar."

"You're not funny."

She shrugged and licked her vanilla custard before it could drip down the cone. "I think I am." She was sitting near the edge of the tailgate. I nudged her hard enough to tip her right off the edge. She landed on her feet, then began to laugh until tears leaked from her eyes. "You really are just you."

I grinned. "I really am. You just know a little bit more

about me, is all. Just like I know you lost your virginity in a treehouse."

"Pinky swear to keep each other's secrets."

I nodded, and we locked pinkies and shook them.

"I'm glad I'm not mad at you anymore." She sat down and licked around the edge of her cone.

"Me too." Frozen custard dripped down my hand. I wiped it away with the puny napkin they'd supplied. "What about you and Buzz?"

"I love him, but I'm hurt. I'm just going to have to decide if I want him in my life more than I wanted him to be truthful with me from the beginning."

"How can you forgive me and not him?"

"I'm not doing the nasty flamingo with you."

I winced. "True story." Friends were easier to forgive than lovers. The expectations were different. "I think having you two over tonight will be a good place to start. Parker can fill you in on what it's been like for him."

"How long has he known?"

"Let's just say that Nick Newton was not mauled by a bobcat."

"Holy crap. You took him out?"

"He had a gun on Parker. He was going to kill him. He

wanted to kill both of us. I will always do everything in my power to defend and protect the people I love."

"Like dragging me out of a five-alarm fire," she said.

"Exactly."

She took one big bite off the top of the melting custard. "Ow," she said, pressing her fingertips to her temple. "Brain freeze."

While she was rubbing her head, Smooshie came up behind her and licked the custard above the cone line clean off. "Smoosh!"

Smooshie licked her forearm as an apology, or Nadine had dripped custard down her arm. I was going to choose the latter.

I saw a guy, the one with the tie from yesterday, enter the side door.

"There," I said to Nadine, pointing with my cone. "That's where the gambling happens. The man that just walked in was playing on one of the machines.

Nadine got up as if to investigate, but Bobby Morris pulled into the drive-in in a blue sedan and parked in an empty spot three vehicles down from us. He got out of the car with two small boys—his sons, I assumed—in tow. He wore a pair of jeans, roughed-up farm boots, and a pale-yellow T-shirt that complimented his dark skin tone. It was weird seeing him out of uniform.

He walked over to us. "I'm on dad duty today. I'm going to get these guys something to eat, and then we can talk."

AS BOBBY'S SONS ATE AT ONE OF THE PICNIC TABLES, NADINE relayed all the information we'd managed to get from Electa Laverty. When she'd finished, she said, "It looks like Sheriff Avery is in this up to his bald patch." She tapped the top of her head for emphasis.

"And what do you want to do about it?" he asked.

"What do you mean? I want to take him down! He is trying to convict Buzz of a murder he didn't commit."

"What motive would Hanley or the sheriff have to kill Jock?"

"Maybe Jock was greedy. Wanted more of the pie for himself. Maybe he threatened to expose them."

"Maybe," Bobby said.

"Whose side are you on here?" Nadine asked. "You gave me the phone reports. You wouldn't have done that if you thought what the sheriff was doing was right."

"I'm on the side of justice and the law. I will go wherever the evidence takes me. But that means I can't bring my own biases into a case. If you get your mind set that a crime is committed by someone, you spend your whole time trying to find evidence that proves your theory. It can make you dismiss evidence that might lead you in another direction."

"Do you think the sheriff is involved?" I asked.

He shrugged. "Maybe. It remains to be seen." Bobby was not only a smart man, but he was also fair. That made him a damn good deputy and an even better investigator. And everything he'd said so far had rung true.

Nadine crossed her arms over her chest. "Does this mean you aren't going to help us?"

"We can't do anything about the sheriff right now," he said calmly as if talking down a bear. "But I promise, if the evidence goes there, Sheriff Avery will be held accountable for his actions."

"When? When Buzz is locked up behind bars for the next twenty years? You know as well as I do that a murder conviction is almost impossible to overturn."

"Can you hold off for just a little longer?"

"Why?" I asked. I put feeling into the word.

Bobby looked around for a moment, then said, "The Missouri Federal Bureau of Investigations approached me six months ago. They're investigating large, regular monthly payments going into a bank account under the sheriff's name. They tasked me with finding out why."

"So, you do think he's corrupt," Nadine snapped. "Then help me."

"If what you're saying about the zoning citations is true, this goes deeper than the sheriff, and I need to know how many players we're talking about if we want to take down everyone involved. If we bring in the sheriff, we'll alert his partners, and they will scatter. What if it was one of *them* that killed Jock? The sheriff, no matter his failings, doesn't strike me as the kind of guy who would try to poison someone with antifreeze then stab them. And he darn sure doesn't strike me as the kind of guy with enough tech savvy to know how to use a spoof app on his phone or disguise his voice. Does he seem like that kind of guy to you?"

Nadine cast her eyes to her lap. "No. I guess not."

"Good. Now stop jumping to the fire with another match. We need to be smart, or whoever is involved is going to walk away unscathed, and neither of us will have a career or a pot to piss in. Okay?"

"Okay," she agreed.

"Do you know about the gambling in town?" I nodded to the drive-in.

He nodded. "That's how the case was brought to the FBI's attention. They got a call about the gaming in town, and the person told them they filed a report, and it was ignored, and that the person had talked to the sheriff directly, and he encouraged this witness to 'let it go.'"

"Do you know who?" I asked.

Bobby shook his head. "I've looked for that report for

months. If it existed, it's gone now. The FBI says that the tipster could give credible testimony, but they need physical evidence of the corruption and the organization behind it."

My phone rang. It was the shelter's number. I raised a finger. "Hold on," I answered. "This is Lily."

"Hey, Lily. My mom called," Keith said. "She says she has that information you wanted. She said if you swing by this afternoon, she'll give it to you."

"Great! Thanks, Keith." I'd asked Keith's mom to keep the information private when I'd called her this morning, even from Keith, and it looked like she had. After I ended the call, I asked Nadine and Bobby, "Who wants to find out who owns Trinity Commercial Real Estate?"

A slow smile spread across their lips as they both raised their hands.

"Let's pack up the kids and head to the courthouse. We're going on a field trip."

CHAPTER 20

Nadine and I dropped Smooshie with Buzz, then headed to the courthouse to meet with Bobby. It turned out that business licenses fell under public information. We were excited to find out who owned Trinity Commercial Realty, and if we could also find out what business properties they leased, we might be able to figure out where all the gaming action was taking place.

"Here you go, sweetheart." Keith's mom, Charlotte "Just call me Charlie" Porter, handed me a stapled stack of filled-out forms. Where Keith was tall and lanky, she was short and robust. She had short brown hair, tasteful makeup applied, and she wore small diamond earrings and a pendant necklace. Her eyes, though, were the same startlingly beautiful shade of aquamarine as Keith's.

Nadine and Bobby peered over my shoulders as I flipped through the pages twice, frustrated when I couldn't find a single name or signature. Trinity Commercial Real Estate was owned by a shell corporation called Honeysuckle Unlimited, LLC. "Why would they register a business with another business?" Nadine asked.

"For lots of reasons, sweetheart," Charlie said. "The legitimate reasons usually involve avoiding litigation or tax shelters. Also, people can use them to maintain anonymity between themselves and a business."

"And what would be the illegitimate reasons," Bobby asked.

"Tax evasion, money laundering, a way to hide money."

"Well, poop on a cracker," Nadine said. "How are we going to find out who owns the dang company?"

Charlie cackled. "You can get a warrant for whatever bank they're with. Banks are required to have real names of shell company owners just in case the records are subpoenaed for cases of financial crime."

Charlie was an intelligent and capable force of nature. "Wow, you really know your stuff."

"Thirty years of filing business registrations and answering some of the oddest questions from our customers." She winked at me. "I was the original search engine. Google before Google was cool."

Keith's mom was fabulous. "I see where Keith gets his awesomeness from. I can't tell you how much we appreciate your help, Charlie."

She beamed with pleasure. "You just did."

As we walked out to the parking lot, the name of the shell company kept playing in my head. *Honeysuckle Limited, LLC*. Why did it seem familiar?

I halted abruptly, and Nadine walked into my back. "Lils, give a girl warning."

"I got it," I said. "Honeysuckle is the key."

"There are a million honeysuckle plants all over Missouri. I'm not sure it helps," Bobby disagreed.

I waved him off. "No. Theresa told me that her dad called her mom Hummingbird. His nickname for her."

Nadine gave me the "hurry up and get to the poin"t hand twirl.

I frowned at her. "She said that Sheriff Avery likes to say that if he hadn't put out the honeysuckle, he'd have never trapped his hummingbird."

My BFF made a face like someone farted. "What does that even mean?"

"It's circumstantial," Bobby said. "Far-fetched, even. It's not even enough to get a warrant."

I clapped them both on the upper arms. "But if he *is* part of this, it might be enough to rattle his cage."

A slow grin formed on Nadine's face as she processed my plan. Finally, she said, "I like the way you think."

"I'm not sure," Bobby said. "It could work, or it could blow up our careers."

"Then you're going to like this part of my plan even more. I'm going to talk to Sheriff Avery alone."

"Or not," Nadine said. "If he killed Jock, he won't hesitate to take you out."

"I really don't think he murdered Jock, because, while I think the man is a royal jerk, I don't think he's stupid. Whoever threw Jock onto The Cat's Meow parking lot was acting on impulse. I don't think Sheriff Avery would do that. However, he might know who did, and he's covering for them."

Bobby shook his head. "I don't know..."

"I'll record the whole thing with my phone, and I'll open a call to you all so you can listen in. Come on. I won't spill the beans about him being investigated. And he knows I'm a nosy freak. I think the only thing that will surprise him about seeing me is that I didn't come sooner."

Nadine nodded her head with a sigh. "She's right," she said to Bobby. "And it's a way to escalate the sheriff without tipping our hand. Even if he doesn't confess, it might force him to contact his partners or make some other stupid mistake that shows his hand."

"Hey, a gambling reference." My excitement spiked as I considered our risky plan. "I like it."

"Come on," Bobby said. As we walked toward the

parking area, he added, "Why do I feel like I'm going to regret this?"

THE FIRST TIME I'D VISITED THE SHERIFF'S STATION, IT HAD been to see Parker. He'd been arrested for a murder he hadn't committed and locked up in jail. Even though I'd only known him a short while, at the time, I'd been determined to save him. I resisted the urge to call Parker before heading into the sheriff's station. He would only worry, and this was going to be a quick in and out.

I walked past the prison fence, remembering the jerk who'd cat-called me, along with Parker's furious reaction. Luckily, it seemed as if it wasn't yard time, so the area was empty of inmates. Nadine had given me one of her light nylon windbreakers with an interior pocket to hide my phone. Bobby had dropped his kids off with his mother, and he and Nadine were waiting in his sedan for me. I glanced at the parking lot. "Can you hear me?" I asked.

The lights on Bobby's car flashed off and on. They had heard me loud and clear.

"I'm going in."

When I reached the front door, I was dismayed at how much my hands trembled. I rubbed my palms against my jeans, clenched my fingers, released them, then gave them a hard shake.

I was doing this, and I wouldn't let Sheriff Avery intimidate me. I also planned to summon up all my magical juju. I wouldn't ask him anything not related to the gambling, the zoning scheme, or the murder, because I wasn't a fan of humiliating anyone by eliciting personal secrets, but as for the rest, this man had it coming.

I walked up to the reception area, a gray-walled room that had changed little in a year and a half. A young officer sat behind a glass exchange, reading his phone. His name tag said Bowles. He glanced at me. "Are you here for visiting hours?"

"No, I'd like to speak to Sheriff Avery."

"The sheriff is not taking visitors today," Deputy Bowles said.

I swallowed and steeled my nerves. "He'll see me. Tell him it's Lily Mason."

The uniformed officer studied me for a second. "He won't see you, Ms. Mason. He put a note on my desk three days ago that says if you show up, I am to send you packing. Immediately."

I expelled the breath I'd been holding. "Tell him I have information about Honeysuckle Unlimited. Go on," I said when he glared at me. "Tell him."

Deputy Bowles reluctantly picked up the phone and relayed my message to whoever he was talking to on the other end. He put the phone down in its cradle. "Just a minute," he said.

It was actually two minutes before the phone on his desk rang. He picked it up. "Yes, sir. Yes. Uh-huh. Yep. Yes. Okay." He hung up and flicked his gaze at me. "I'll ring you in." He gestured to the door at the far end of the room. I had programmed the volume button to trigger the recording, so I started it before I strolled to the other end of the reception. When I made it there, a loud buzzer sound startled me, but the lock unclicked. I went inside.

The room was filled with a dozen or more cubicles with computers and two chairs at each one. Sheriff Avery, large and in charge, stood outside his office with his arms crossed and an expression of pure annoyance on his face.

"This is about to get really fun," I said out loud for my compadres in the parking lot.

The sheriff gave me a get-in-here wave then headed into his office. I followed him in.

"Close the door behind you," he said.

"Hello, Sheriff Avery," I greeted.

His neck was red and blotchy. Nerves. "I don't have time for niceties, Ms. Mason." He pulled at his collar. "Get to your point."

"Trinity Commercial Real Estate," I stated.

"I don't know what you're talking about," he said.

Ping. Lie. "I know you, Jock, and Clem Hanley were in a partnership. Buying then leasing commercial property, then setting them up for illegal gambling." I was really tossing the crap around now, but I hoped I'd guessed enough to make him unsettled enough to screw up.

"I don't have any idea what you're talking about."

Another lie. "Honeysuckle," I said. "You wouldn't have caught your hummingbird without it."

He blustered, his face turning an alarming shade of crimson. "Now, you just hold on there, young miss!"

I let my cougar awaken inside me. A little dangerous with the full moon only one night away, but I risked it anyway for the extra boost it gave to my senses and my magic. His heartbeat was rapid, his blood pressure elevated, his breathing erratic. In other words, he was definitely rattled.

"Did you kill Jock Simmons?"

"No," he rasped.

"Are you covering for someone who did?"

He shook his head. "I don't know who killed Jock."

"But you know it isn't Buzz. You are working extra hard to hide evidence. Like the suspicious phone call that sent Buzz to the diner in the first place."

"I don't know who did it," he said.

Again, this was the truth. Crappola. "Then why are you refusing to look at any other suspects? Are you trying to protect Theresa?"

His eyes flicked toward the family photo of him, Theresa, and Anna.

"Anna?" I asked. I pushed all my magic into the question. "Do you think Anna is involved?"

Avery roared, shoving back his chair as he stood up from the desk. His resistance was strong. Whatever the secret, he didn't want it known. "You nosy little—" He shook a fist at me. "I ought to throw you in jail with your freak of a cousin. Both of you are nothing but trouble!"

I stood up to face him. "Is Anna involved in Hanley and Jock's real estate and gambling scheme?" I pressed. Theresa had said her mother was in the business honor society at her university. She had the brains to pull it off. "Is she neck deep in all this corruption? Are you covering for her?"

For a brief moment, the blood drained from his face. He flopped back into his chair. "It was me," he lied, and I know because my magic was pinging like crazy. "I did it. I killed Jock, I set up the gambling, I did it."

His emotional confession rocked me to my core. He was desperate, despondent, and throwing himself on the proverbial sword for someone else.

"What about Hanley and Jock?"

"Jock was in on it with me. I killed him because he threatened Theresa. I used antifreeze over a couple of days then stabbed him with a filet knife."

Lies, lies, and more lies.

"Tell me the truth," I demanded.

He gaped at me, then opened his desk and pulled out a gun. Two uniformed men were standing in the open door to the sheriff's office. They were goggling at Avery. They'd heard it all. They'd heard his confession. *Fuu-uddge.*

"You have to leave, Ms. Mason," one of the men said. "Now. Go."

Oh, Goddess, I'd pushed him too far. "Call Theresa," I said loudly. "Call her now and tell her to call me!"

"What are you doing?" the sheriff seethed. He pointed the gun at me. "I will shoot you, Ms. Mason."

It was a lie.

"After, I'll shoot myself and laugh all the way to hell."

The part about shooting himself rang true. He was not only going to take the fall for his wife, but he was also going to take himself out of the equation. "Don't. Please. Killing yourself is not the answer."

His pulse was dangerously high now as he lived and breathed fight or flight. My phone vibrated. I pulled it out of my pocket and put it on speaker.

"Hello," Theresa said. "Lily?"

"Think about your daughter. Your wife. They won't come back from this. Not easily."

"What's going on?" Theresa asked. "Daddy?"

His face paled again, and the gun lowered a little.

"Put the gun down, Sheriff," one of the officers said. "Nobody needs to get hurt here."

"A gun? Lily, tell me what's going on?" Theresa asked.

"Just a little misunderstanding," I told her.

Avery glared at me for a moment, then all the anger drained from him. "Goodbye, Theresa. Tell your mother I love her."

Not today. I was already Shifter-jazzed, so it didn't take much for me to leap the distance between us. I flew over his desk with faster-than-human speed and tackled the sheriff before he could put the gun to his head. The weapon dropped to the floor as I clung to him.

"Lily!" Nadine exclaimed, the fear thick in her voice.

A quick peek around the room showed me Nadine was at the door now, along with Bobby. The two other officers were stunned in place.

I focused my predatorial gaze on Sheriff Avery.

"Your eyes," he whispered. "What's wrong with your eyes?"

I closed them, willing my cougar back into her box. When I opened them again, I knew by the surprise on his face that the bright green of them had faded to a darker hue. I shook my head at him. "I think you're under arrest."

Bobby and Nadine plucked me off the sheriff, and I heard one of the deputies say, "You have the right to remain silent," as they helped him to his feet.

CHAPTER 21

"Everything smells absolutely delicious," I gushed. The scent of red sauce, sausage, garlic bread, ricotta, Romano, and parmesan cheeses filled the air. I was taking the enthusiasm to an eleven, but I hated everyone being mad at me. I'd been berated by Buzz, Nadine, Bobby, and Parker for putting myself in danger. The only one who hadn't yelled at me was Smooshie, but she must have sensed something was wrong because she'd wedged her big body between my knees and put her head in my lap fifteen minutes earlier, and she hadn't moved since.

Parker's anxiety level was up as well, because Elvis had glued himself to Parker's hip.

"I'm sorry I upset you," I said again. "I couldn't let him kill himself. Not when I knew I could stop him."

"And get yourself shot in the process. You may be quick, Lily, but bullets are quicker. And what if you had exposed your Shifter side? You have warned me multiple times what might happen if people found out about your kind. You're not just putting yourself in danger."

I sighed. He was right. I shouldn't have used so much of my second nature. As it was, the deputies had written off my super-human leap to the adrenaline rush of the situation. "I don't want to fight with you."

"You have no idea how much I love you," he snarled. "If you did, you wouldn't go out of your way to get yourself hurt."

"I love you, too, Parker. But it's not in my nature to back down when I have a friend in need."

"Avery is not your friend."

"No, but Theresa is. You expected me to sit there and watch her father kill himself? I pushed him to it. I used my magic, and I pushed him to tell me something he would rather die than divulge. I had a responsibility to stop it."

He threw the slotted spoon into the red sauce pan then slumped against the counter. "God, you make me crazy."

I stood up and approached him. "Parker." He met my gaze. "I am who I am. I can't promise I won't put myself in danger again. You've known me for less than two years. How many times have I been shot at? I'm not sure why you're acting like this is something new."

"Because this time I wasn't with you. When Nadine called me, I felt…helpless."

I let my kitty bleed into my eyes, flashing him with my brights. "*I'm* not helpless. I don't need to be rescued. That's not the kind of relationship I want with you."

"Then what kind do you want?"

"The kind we have every day when I'm not in danger. The kind where we trust each other to be true to our natures."

"My nature can get erratic." The corner of his mouth tugged up in a half-smile.

"Mine can too. I guess we're a perfect match." I leaned into Parker and kissed him. "Are we friends again?"

"Yes," he said. "Friends, again."

"Good." I pushed myself up straight. "I'll set the table."

"We're here!" I heard Nadine holler from the doorway.

Smooshie gave a short, sharp, alert bark. "Just in time," Parker said. "Our guests have arrived."

I poked my head out of the kitchen and yelled, "Come on back!"

Buzz and Nadine strode on in, Nadine holding lemon-lime soda and Buzz carrying a bottle of gin. "We brought the party," Nadine said.

Buzz kissed my cheek. "Hey, kiddo."

"Ice is in the freezer." I pointed to a cabinet. "Cups are up there." I smiled. "But I'll take a beer."

Parker chuckled. "That's my girl."

"Well," Nadine said. "The feds came and got Sheriff Avery. They are bringing him up on charges of racketeering. They obtained a warrant to get the name of the Honeysuckle Unlimited, LLC business because they don't believe he was in it alone."

"I don't believe he was in on it at all," I said.

Nadine set a cold beer in front of me. "Why do you say that? He confessed."

"And he was lying," I told her. "You know I know when someone is being dishonest. He's covering for someone, and that's going to come out when they subpoena the bank records."

"Who would he cover for?"

"His wife, Anna. I think she was in on this real estate scheme with Jock and Hanley."

Nadine sat down in the chair near me. "Christ."

"Yep." I glanced at Buzz. He had really aged in the past few weeks. "I think you should shift with me tomorrow night."

He curled his lip. "Mind your business," he said.

"It *is* my business. If you're trying to strip down human DNA, you have to remember, in the human world, at your age, you'd be ready for the retirement home, and I hate to say it, but you've aged a decade in the past month. I'm not sure how many decades you can afford to lose." I tried to keep my tone light and teasing, but I had real fear for my uncle.

"Did you invite me over for a lecture? Or to eat?"

"Can't it be both?"

Nadine had grown really quiet, and Parker said, "Nadine, how do you feel about Buzz suppressing his nature. Is this what you want?"

"I don't need therapy," Buzz said. "I'm doing this, and that's that."

Nadine teared up. "I hate what this is doing to you, Buzz. All we do is fight all the time. I miss you. I miss the way you were before you stopped being you."

"You want a baby. We talked about this."

"Before I knew what kind of toll it would take on you," she fired back. "We can adopt. We can pick a sperm donor. Hell, we can live our lives together without any children. I don't want you doing this just for me. I'm worried it's damaging you."

"Women have gone through much worse to conceive. Getting daily hormone shots for in-vitro fertilization, risking high blood pressure, chronic headaches, mood swings, weight gain, nausea, vomiting, and all this for months and months before getting several eggs implanted in their uterus. Then when they finally start to feel better, they have to deal with pregnancy on top of it. Are you saying that it's okay for a woman to sacrifice to have children, but it's not all right for me?"

"Dang, Buzz," I said, feeling the passion and conviction behind his words. "You really want this, don't you? You want a child of your own." I'd just gotten on to Parker about how I could make my own decisions. Maybe it was my turn to stop trying to control the situation.

"I do," he said. He cast a stark gaze at Nadine. "I want it more than I've wanted anything in my life."

"You're not just doing it for me, then?" Nadine asked.

"I'm doing it for us," Buzz replied. He went to her and dropped to his knees beside Nadine's chair. "I want you to have my baby, Nadine Jennifer Booth. Can you put up with me aging and getting really crotchety for a couple more months?"

"Buzz, I'd put up with you for the rest of my life." She wrapped her arms around his neck, and he hugged her waist.

I cast a sideways glance at Parker. *Awkward,* I mouthed.

He winked. *Counseling works,* he mouthed back.

I stuck my tongue out at him.

Unexpectedly, the room filled with noxious fumes. "Oh, Gosh," Nadine gasped. She plugged her nose. "Ugh. I can taste it."

Smooshie was under the table, lying down with her head on her paws. "Smoosh? Not again." I waved my hand around, and Parker opened the back door to air the kitchen. She twitched her ears as if to say, not me.

"I think it's Elvis," Parker said. The giant gas machine was on his bed in the corner of the kitchen. Parker walked over and made a face. "It's stronger over here."

"Oh man, get him outside," I complained. "It smells like he ate a few dozen rotten eggs."

"Poor baby," Parker said. "Nobody loves a stinky boy."

When he took the dogs out—plural, because Smooshie got up and joined them—Buzz stood up and announced, "Ladies and gentlemen, Elvis has left the building."

AFTER DINNER, WE ALL WENT AND SAT IN CHAIRS AROUND A fire pit we'd thrown together with a tractor tire metal rim in Parker's backyard. Parker had bought marshmallows, chocolate bars, and graham crackers.

"S'mores don't pair well with gin and soda," Buzz said as his marshmallow caught on fire.

"I beg to differ." Nadine took her perfectly roasted marshmallow off the stick and mashed it between two crackers and a square of chocolate. "S'mores pair with everything." In her tipsy state, she dropped the well-made smore right into the fire.

We all laughed.

She pouted. "It was so perfect!" She turned to me. "Can I see?" she asked.

"See what?"

"You know." She widened her eyes. "I want to see you turn into a cat. Buzz can't do it, but you can. I *really* want to see."

I leaned back to catch Buzz's eye. He seemed to consider the consequences for a few seconds, then nodded his head. "If you're okay with it," he said.

"I can't do it out here," I told her. "Someone might see."

"In the house?" She giggled. "You are housebroken, right?"

"I'm going to take your gin away," I told her.

"Noooo," she whined. "Not the gin."

I laughed. "Come on. We'll do it in the bedroom."

Nadine winked at Buzz. "Did you hear that? We're going to do it in the bedroom."

"No one does the nasty flamingo in the bedroom but me," Parker said.

"And usually by himself," Buzz said.

We all laughed.

Nadine followed me into the house and down the hall to

the master bedroom. Other than the living room, it had the most floor space. "Sit on the bed," I told her. "And please don't freak out."

"I won't," she said. Her hiccup after her statement didn't instill a lot of confidence in me.

I stripped my shirt off.

"Why are you taking off your clothes?"

"Have you ever seen a cat in a bag? Well, that's what it's like to shift with clothing on." And really, I'd been getting naked and shifting around other Shifters from a really young age, so I wasn't body conscious. The fact that she asked though made me a little nervous. Humans could be weird about nudity.

She whistled, low and slow. "That makes so much sense. You know," she said, "I'm really glad you didn't die today."

"I'm really glad too."

"You're brave, Lily."

"So, are you."

"No, I'm not." She gave me a tight smile. "But I'm trying."

When I took off the last of my clothes, Nadine started chanting, "Shift, shift, shift," while bouncing on the end of the bed.

Awesome.

I held my hand up in the air like a Vegas showgirl, snapped my fingers, just to make it fancy, then called forth my beast. Fur sprouted across my skin, my face narrowed, my nose and mouth protruding forward as my ears moved up on my head. I watched the fascination in Nadine's expression as it reflected many spectrums of emotions, from fear, amazement, wonder, and finally, judging by the smile on her face and the tears in her eyes, pure joy.

I was fully a cougar now, and I waited for her to make the first move.

"Lily," she said after a minute or so of gaping at me. "You're beautiful. Can I pet you?"

I made a little rawr sound, then began to purr when I put my face near her leg, and she stroked the fur between my ears.

She giggled. "You're like a giant tabby."

I gave her hand a playful nip. She snatched back and giggled some more.

I let her pet me for a while until Smooshie began to whine from behind the closed door. My sweet baby was feeling left out!

I walked to where I'd placed my clothes, and I shifted back.

After I dressed, Nadine embraced me. "Thank you, Lily."

"For what?"

"For helping me. For being the best friend I've ever had. I don't know what I'd do without you."

Parker knocked. "Hey, are you decent?"

"I'm never decent," Nadine boasted.

"Come in," I said.

Parker opened the door. "The Blakes are getting Hester back tomorrow morning. We need to do a quick inspection of the property in the morning before she comes back to make sure there aren't any more toxins around the yard."

"Okay," I said, wondering why he was telling me this now.

"Theresa had said she would do it, but she called just a bit ago and told me she can't make it...for obvious family stuff. Can you handle it on your own? I have to get stuff ready for the volunteers coming to help me put up fence tomorrow, or I would do it."

A wave of sadness passed through me for Theresa. Her life had been turned upside down for the umpteenth time. I knew what it was like to have that kind of luck. "I'll do it."

Nadine leaned into me. "If you want, I can come with you."

"Girl, you are going to be hungover. Do you really want to get up at the crack of dawn on your day off for two days in a row?"

"No," she said. "Not really."

"That's what I thought." I sighed. "How did Theresa sound?"

Parker shook his head. "About as expected. I hate that she's going through this. She's a really good person, even if her parents aren't."

I worried about Theresa. Parker was right, she was a good person, and she deserved some happiness after all the crap life had put her through. I just hoped, eventually, she would forgive me for my part in blowing up her life.

CHAPTER 22

M ick and Veronica Blake lived in the Sycamore Valley subdivision north of town. I'd never been to their house before, because Parker and Theresa had vetted them years ago, and Theresa usually took care of the home visits. I wanted to call Theresa to tell her how sorry I was she was going through another crisis. She had been strong enough to get through years of Jock's abuse and come out on the other side with her humor and warmth intact. The fact that she'd been able to trust in love again with Keith had seemed like a miracle to me. I admired her, and I didn't want to lose her friendship.

The houses in the subdivision were similar in architecture, almost all of them split-levels with two-car garages, apart from a few ranch-style homes on three of the corners. The Blakes lived in a gray-blue split-level with midnight-blue trim and shutters. The door had been painted the same accent color. I walked up the steps and knocked on the door.

Veronica answered. "Hi, Lily," she said, a bright smile on her round, almost cherubic face. "Come on in." She had thick tawny hair that hung down past her shoulders.

"Thanks." I went inside, and we walked up a set of carpeted steps to the main floor. The house was clean, the furniture plushy but worn. There was a large dog bed taking up space between the recliner and the couch.

Veronica said, "We both like being able to pet the dogs we care for when we watch television." She laughed. "Of course, Hester spends most of her time on Mick's lap in the recliner. I told him he was going to need a bigger chair to fit both of their butts."

I knew they didn't have any other pets, which made them perfect for fostering pit bulls who needed to be in single-pet homes. Veronica was a website designer and worked from home, and her husband Mick was a plumber. He'd done all the plumbing at the new shelter at cost. It had saved us a bundle of money. Mick and Parker had become friends when he hired Mick to do the plumbing on the current shelter. He'd talked the couple into fostering three years ago. While they'd been reluctant at first, they'd turned out to be amazing at it. Hester was their fifth foster dog. The first four had all been adopted within a few months.

"Hester is lucky to be with you while she waits for her forever family."

"She's such a sweetheart. We've been the lucky ones." She

gestured toward the kitchen. "I'll let you get to it. If you have any questions, I'll be back in my office. It's just the first door on the left in the hall."

"Thanks. It shouldn't take too long." All I needed to do was check the house and the yard to make sure there wasn't anything hazardous for the dog, like poisonous plants, pins, needles, unruly electrical cords, toxins, and other dangerous objects.

I made quick work of the interior inspection. The Blakes had done a great job of making the home pet-friendly. They even turned one entire bedroom space into a doggy haven, with a futon mattress on the floor, toys to play with, and a TV mounted high on the wall.

Veronica came out of her office and joined me in the dog room. "Hester likes to have the television on when I have to leave the house to shop and stuff." She smiled wistfully. "Her favorite program is *Golden Girls*. She always wags her tail when Rose is on screen."

"You all have made a lovely and safe space for her and the other dogs you've cared for."

"I can't wait to pick her up from the vet today. Dr. Petry says she's going to be just fine." She pulled a tissue from her pocket and dabbed at her eyes. "I've never been so scared in all my life. Where in the world did she get ahold of antifreeze? We didn't have any here, not even in the garage. When Parker said someone might have deliberately poisoned her, we checked the backyard, which is the only place she could have come into contact with it, and we couldn't find anything."

"This wasn't your fault." She walked with me back out to the living room. "The house is good to go. I'll go check out the backyard and then around the front. It shouldn't take too long."

"Great," Veronica said, "because Mick is waiting in the parking lot of Petry's Pet Clinic to pick Hester up and bring her home."

I arched a brow at the way she said home. "Are you and Mick considering adopting Hester?"

She shook her head, then nodded. "I can't help it. I just love her so much. She's a complete cuddle monster. I think I knew from the first night we brought her home that I wanted to keep her, but we've been reluctant to make it official because it means giving up on the pit bulls who can't be placed in homes with other pets."

I knew what love at first sight felt like. I'd had it with Smooshie when she'd tackled me out of the way of an oncoming car. She'd been my loyal companion ever since.

I hugged Veronica. "I love a good foster fail," I said, and we both laughed through tears. I patted her back. "Let me go check out the rest of the property so we can get your baby home."

The back deck was large, no loose nails or screws. The steps were in good repair leading down to the yard. There was a five-foot chain-link fence surrounding the yard, with a gap that looked to be about eight inches from the neighbors' fences on either side. The neighbor to the left had a swing set and a trampoline in the backyard. The neighbor on the right had an elaborate art installation above a water fountain that featured metal sheets cut and twisted into flames and painted in yellow and orange, above the flames, an orange bird, sitting on a yellow perch with a heart painted in red below its claws, its wings spread, ready to fly.

The sliding glass door opened, and Veronica joined me on the deck. "It's haunting, isn't it?"

"It's a phoenix, right?"

"I think so. My neighbor Patty, her husband died a year ago." She shook her head somberly, and in a quieter voice said, "He killed himself."

"That's awful."

"Patty, understandably, had a difficult time, so her daughter moved back home to stay with her for a while. Her daughter made the metal sculpture. She said the bird is her father, flying free, the ribbon with the heart is for the family he left behind, and the flames are reserved for the people who drove him to his death." She shuddered. "It's all a little ghastly for my taste, but everyone grieves in their own ways."

"Why did he kill himself?"

"Apparently, he'd put them in enough debt that Patty had to sell their business to pay it off."

"Wow. It makes me thankful for the things I have."

"Same. David was a Chamber of Commerce board member, and when I started my home business, he organized an article in the local newspaper for me. He was a nice man. It's a damn shame." She patted my arm. "I'll let you get back to it."

The freshly cut lawn was clear of weeds and debris. I went down the steps and walked the perimeter of the fence. The left side and the back fence were clear, but as I walked down the right side, there was a muddy space between the fences, and it looked like Hester or another dog had started to dig under it.

I knelt down and leaned in for a closer look. The ground was saturated. I reached under the fence and dragged my finger through the wet soil then inhaled the scent of it. The aroma was watered down, but it was sweet and chemical-like at the same time. This had to be where the antifreeze had been given to Hester, but it looked like someone had doused it with a copious amount of water to dilute it.

I looked at the neighbor's yard. Could Patty or her daughter have poisoned Hester? Why? My skin itched as fury simmered just below the surface.

I understood that tragedy could make a person lash out, but to harm an animal or any living creature to make yourself feel better was monstrous. They couldn't get away with it.

I marched up the fence line, through the gate, and up the steps to the neighbor's house.

The cougar raged to get out and exact vengeance. Down, girl, I chided myself. Between staying at Parker's most the time, which meant less shifting, and the full moon tonight, I was seriously on edge. I resisted the urge to pound the door down. Instead, I poked the doorbell over and over with what I considered incredible restraint.

"Just a minute!" a woman yelled. "Stop ringing the damn doorbell."

I did not stop ringing the doorbell. In fact, I poked it four more times in rapid succession.

The front door flew open.

Jordan Deeter stood in front of me, wearing a blue hoody that said, "Tornadoes will blow you away." Tornadoes were the Two Hills Community College sports mascot.

She hadn't expected to see me any more than I'd expected to see her. We were both stunned silent.

Finally, she spoke first. "Hi." She frowned at me. "What are you doing here? And how do you know where I live?"

"I didn't know this was your house," I said, my mouth suddenly dry. My emotions were clouded by confusion.

"I was doing the inspection at the Blakes' home. Hester is being released today."

Jordan nibbled at her upper lip. "I'm glad she's going to be okay."

"I think you better invite me in," I said.

She shook her head. "Mom's asleep."

"Then we can have this conversation right here on the porch where all your neighbors can hear about how you poisoned a defenseless dog."

Her nose twitched, but she nodded. "We can talk privately in my studio in the basement. There's an entrance by the garage."

"All right." I ushered her past me. "Lead the way." I followed her down the front steps to the door next to the garage. She punched in a four-digit code: 0507. The lock clicked, and we went inside.

The musty, chilly basement was unfinished with concrete floors, open ceiling, and drywall that hadn't been taped or mudded. A buzzing refrigerator was against the far wall. The ductwork in the open ceiling rattled as air was forced through the vents. Since the basement was so cold, I guessed the central air conditioner was running. There were several metal tables set up, and various-shaped lumps were covered with opaque plastic wrap. Even if there weren't dried splotches of white, dusty matter, I would have guessed it was clay because of the smell.

"I didn't mean to harm Hester," Jordan said. "I would never. Not on purpose."

"Then how did the antifreeze end up over the fence? It was too far away from anything to be an accidental spill."

"I don't know how to explain it." She looked genuinely upset. "But it really *was* an accident."

She was telling the truth, which eased some of my agitation. "Okay," I said. "But why didn't you just say something?"

"I really love volunteering! Helping those dogs and my art are the only thing that gives my life meaning."

The sculpture in the yard, the one commemorating her father's suicide, had been her creation. When I'd asked about her parents, no wonder she'd been so vague. Suicide was hard to talk about. The survivors had to live with the consequences.

"I'm sorry I got so mad. People make mistakes. Goddess knows I have."

"That's really generous," Jordan said. "Thank you."

The clay lumps under the plastic intrigued me. "Can I see some of your work?"

"Sure." She smiled. "I'd love to show you." She pulled the wrap off one of the pieces. It looked like the beginnings of a face. "It's going to be a tribute to my mother," Jordan said.

I moved in close, admiring the detailed lines, and the fact that the one finished eye, even though it was without color or shading, held a depth of life to it that I'd never seen. Of course, I didn't get to a lot of museums. I could see why her work had been chosen to be displayed at the college, though. Jordan was the real deal.

"This is magnificent," I told her.

"Thank you. Do you want something to drink? I have cranberry juice in the fridge."

"No, thanks. I need to get back over to the Blakes and finish up my inspection so they can bring Hester home." An open box with sculpting tools on the other side of the clay caught my attention. It had wire brushes, a looped wire triangle and circle with wooden handles, flat blades, ice-pick-looking tools, several curved instruments in different sizes and different edges, a spearhead knife, and a knife that looked like a curved scalpel.

"These are neat," I said. "It must be fun to work with your hands."

"It's therapeutic," Jordan said.

A glint of light caught my eye and drew my gaze. On a shelf full of ceramics, finished and unfinished, was a bottle of vodka.

I blinked. Oh. Oh, no.

Cranberry juice, vodka, curved scalpel, the exact right

size for Jock's wound. And I had my suspicions about the why. "How did your dad lose his money?"

"Gambling addiction," Jordan said from right behind me. Between the rattling duct and the noisy fridge, I hadn't heard her approach.

Before I could whip around, something hard slammed against my head and drove me to my knees. She served me one more crack on the head before I could shake the first blow, and I blacked out.

CHAPTER 23

My head pounded, and my eyes felt as if they would explode as I blinked them open. The room was noisy with what sounded like the white noise machine I sometimes slept with at home, and it was dark as pitch. I couldn't see a thing. A pungent, overwhelming scent of vinegar made me gag. I tried to use my arms to push myself up from a cold hardwood floor, but I couldn't move them.

I felt sick to my stomach as I maneuvered onto my side and used the wall to sit up. My hands and wrists were bound, prayer-style, behind my back, and my ankles and knees were taped with what felt like duct tape. It took me a few moments to shake the shock and orient to my current reality.

Jordan had hit me in the head. Twice. Maybe more for all I knew. It felt as if she'd taken a hammer to my skull. I tried to bring my cougar forward, which would be the easiest way to slip my bonds, but, alarmingly, I couldn't feel her. Had the blows damaged my ability to change forms?

I tried to wiggle and squirm my way out, but she'd used a lot of tape. I fought the panic clawing at my throat. The idea that I couldn't shift scared me more than being tied up by a crazed co-ed.

The temperature of the room chilled me to the bone. It had to be under forty degrees. As a Shifter, I could take a lot of temperature extremes, so it had to be abnormally cold in the room, but for some reason, my internal heater wasn't working either. I rolled to my side then used my head against the wall to get into an upright sitting position. I drew my knees up in front of me and used my legs to push myself up on the wall.

Why was Jordan doing this?

Gambling addiction. That was the last words I'd heard her say. Did she hold Jock responsible for her dad's death? Is that why she'd killed him? But why wait so long after the fact? She had been a genuinely nice person. I knew she cared about the dogs. Something had to have made her snap.

When I managed to stand up straight, I used the wall as a guide and hopped sideways, feeling for a light switch. It took me several minutes, but I found it.

Goddess, I wish I hadn't.

After the initial blinding, I saw a queen-size bed in the center of the room. On top of the quilted comforter was a dark-haired woman, middle-aged, maybe. And she was absolutely dead. It was hard to tell how long. The cold room had probably slowed down decomposition, and all I could smell was vinegar. The room had a window, and it was painted black. I bounced forward, determined to throw myself out the window if that's what it took to get free.

I cried out when my toe caught on something, and I tripped, falling on my side, landing on top of a large Mason jar full of vinegar. The jar shattered around me, the shards cutting into my shoulder and upper arm, and the vinegar splashed into the open wounds, intensifying the pain.

"Noooo," I whimpered then gagged on the smell again. I saw that there were at least four more jars of the stuff on the floor in the room. This was a freaking nightmare.

I tried to shift again and got no response. I couldn't stop thinking about Parker and Smooshie. What if I never saw them again? What if this was it? Witches and shifters hadn't been able to kill me, neither had gun-toting killers, or a desperate sheriff. Nope. I was going to be taken out by an art major.

Calm down, I told myself. Thinking about all the things I had to lose wasn't going to get me free. I tried to roll up, but broken glass bit into my arm. It gave me an idea. After a two second cuss-fest, I rolled onto my back over the glass. If I could get a piece in my hand, maybe I could cut the bindings. Jordan had done a diligent job with her duct tape. I could wiggle my fingers, but my palms were bound together prayer-style and separate from my wrists.

I managed to get a piece of the broken jar between my fingers, but I'd cut myself, and between the blood and stinging vinegar, I couldn't keep the dang thing from slipping when I tried to saw the tape. I used all my strength to try and stretch the duct tape, but, Goddess in a tutu, the people who had invented the stuff had made a durable product. I managed to pick up the glass piece again, then rolled onto my stomach. I dropped the shard on my butt then wiped my fingers on my jeans to dry them before trying again.

A small ripping sound made my insides dance with triumph. I kept working at it for what seemed like an hour, and I finally freed my palms. It gave me a little more wiggle room, so I bent my knees and brought my ankles to my rear and had another surge of hope when I found I could easily reach them with my hands. I began sawing, working hard to ignore the cramp forming in my thigh.

Cripes. I had to get out of here. No one knew where I was. They wouldn't be worried. I was on my own here, no Parker, Buzz, or Nadine coming to my rescue. I can rescue myself. That's what I'd told Parker the night before. "You can," I said out loud. "You can do this. Rescue yourself."

I got through the ankle tape. Even with my knees still bound, once I got myself up from the floor, I could hobble. I tried the handle on the door, but it was locked from the outside. The window seemed my only option, but when I threw myself at it, I found it wasn't glass, but painted plexiglass.

Okay, first thing was first. I needed to get my hands in front of me. I squatted down and put my bottom through my arms so that my bound wrists were between my calves and thighs. Next, I sat down, then raised my legs and lifted my arms up and over my feet. Yes! Harry Houdini, eat your heart out. I still needed to get my ankles and wrists free, but I was in much better shape than I had been when I'd regained consciousness.

I made short work of my knees by picking at the tape then unrolling it. It hadn't been easy because, like I said, those guys knew how to make tape, but it was still quicker than trying to cut the multi-layers with smooth glass. My teeth chattered as cold air blew constantly from the room vents.

With my knees free and my hands out in front of me, it was easy to get up and explore the room. I tried pulling the plexiglass from the window, but Jordan had screwed it into the frame.

I shivered as the arctic breeze blew against my wet skin. I pulled some nightgowns out of the dresser and covered the vents as best I could to warm up the room. I went to the bedside stand and pulled the drawer open, hoping for a pair of scissors or a knife. Something to get my wrists undone. On the bedside stand was a wedding photo. The custom frame said *David and Patricia Deeter. 5/07/1994*

This was Jordan's parents. They both looked happy in the picture. The idea they were both dead now, leaving Jordan on her own, saddened me. I knew what it was like to be an orphan at such a young age.

"My mom died on their twenty-fifth wedding anniversary," Jordan said.

I staggered in surprise. "That's a really quiet door."

She gave me a tight smile. "I'm sorry, Lily. I like you, but I can't let you go. Not until I've made them pay." She held up a mini handgun. Goddess, why did everyone have a gun?

"Do you plan to kill me?"

"Not if you don't give me any trouble. Once Clem Hanley is dead, then I don't care what happens to me."

"What about your mom?" I gestured to the bed. "That's her, right?"

Jordan nodded. "She took pills. I found her on the seventh."

"That was almost two weeks ago."

"She left me a letter. My dad, Clem Hanley, and Jock Simmons had started a gaming operation in Moonrise and a few towns close by, but Dad developed a taste for gambling. They used his debt against him and forced him out of the business, and when his debt grew beyond his means, they forced him to sell the florist shop to them for half the value. He'd been doing online gambling and going to the boat in Cape Girardeau as well, and when the legitimate creditors started coming after him, he declared bankruptcy then hung himself the day after their anniversary. He'd wanted to spend one more with her before he died. Mom didn't want to spend another one without *him*."

"My parents were both killed when I was seventeen," I said. "I know what it's like to lose the two people who love you most."

"If they loved me the most they would have stuck around," she replied.

"So, for revenge, you poisoned Jock with antifreeze. How did you manage that?" I asked, trying to keep her talking because talking meant she wasn't shooting me.

"The only thing Jock liked more than young women was vodka and cranberry juice cocktails. So, I started an affair with him a few days after mom died."

"You brought him here?"

"My bedroom is the only finished room in the basement, so I never let him up in the main house. Even knowing who my father was, that he was responsible for his death, Jock never had any problems taking me to bed. The man had no conscience." Her hands shook, the gun wagging as she told the story. I think it was a story she'd wanted to tell for a while. "James is going to bring his father to me tonight, and then, I'll be finished."

Was she planning suicide as well? She must have seen

the question on my face, because she said, "No. I plan to turn myself in. I want the whole world to know what they did to my parents. I want to see the faces of all the people in town who let those bastards get away with murder."

"Only they didn't murder your parents. You said so yourself."

Her voice went sharp and cold as she punctuated the air by thrusting the barrel of the gun at me. "If you force someone into a position where the only way out is death, then you have to take some responsibility."

I raised my bound wrists. "I'm not trying to upset you. How is James going to get his father over here? Is he in on the plan with you?"

"He's in love with me. He has been for years, and he hates his dad. But no, James doesn't know what I've planned. He thinks it's a prank. That I just mean to scare his dad."

And that's why she'd been hanging out with James.

"Now," she said. "I need you to come over here and lay on the floor so I can rewrap your arms and legs. I don't want to shoot you, but I will."

When she'd said she didn't want to kill me earlier, she'd meant it, but just now, when she said she'd shoot me, she'd meant that, too.

I heard distinct barking sounds outside the window.

Smooshie? My pulse spiked, but I worked to slow it down to conserve my energy and strength.

Jordan's brow furrowed at the noise. I took a step toward her. "Don't move," she ordered me. "I *will* shoot you."

"I've survived worse," I said, taking another step in her direction.

She jerked the gun at me, her finger sliding to the trigger. "Stop!"

The doorbell rang. When Jordan reflexively turned to look over her shoulder, I lunged at her, a primal scream tearing from my throat as I rammed my shoulder into her chest. She shouted, her gun hand flying up, and she fired the weapon into the ceiling. Before she could bring the gun down again, I clasped my hands and swung both my arms like I was holding a bat and clocked her under the chin. Jordan's head hit the doorframe.

I wrapped my bound wrists behind her head and pulled her face down on my knee then threw her aside. She'd dropped the gun, so I picked it up before sprinting past her down the hallway to the living room.

I heard Jordan wail from her mother's bedroom as I unbolted the front door and flung it open. Parker's face was red with sweat and terror as he fell inside. He'd been trying to beat down the door to get to me. Smooshie rammed her body around him, growling and snarling until I dropped to the floor beside her.

Parker knelt beside me, his hands and eyes searching me for injuries beyond the cuts and bruises.

"Call the police," I said when I could breathe.

"I already did." I heard sirens in the distance as if they'd been cued. He gave me an odd look. "Why didn't you go all furry?"

"Something's wrong with me. I was hit on the head, and when I woke up, I couldn't reach my cougar side. It doesn't matter right now." I handed him the gun. "Jordan is down the hall. You have to go keep an eye on her until the police get here. Make sure she doesn't hurt herself."

"I don't want to leave you alone."

Smooshie was practically on top of me. "I'm not alone." I touched his leg. "Thanks for finding me."

Parker shook his head as he headed down the hall. "When Veronica called and said you'd disappeared four hours ago, but your truck was still out front, I was frantic. Smooshie tracked you to this house. She's a real hero."

I kissed my fur baby's nose. "Such a good Smooshie." She licked my neck then made a yuck face. "Vinegar," I told her. "I feel the same way."

Parker walked back into the living room with Jordan in tow, his face ashen and haunted.

"Whoops," I said. "I guess I should have mentioned the dead mom in the room."

EPILOGUE

Bobby Morris, who had been appointed acting sheriff, arrived with backup. One of the deputies had cut my wrists free. Parker and I gave our statements while they arrested Jordan and took her into custody. A morgue van was called for the body, and Bobby insisted I go to the hospital to have my wounds looked at, so Parker took me to the emergency room, where they put fourteen stitches into my right shoulder wound and glued a deeper, but smaller gouge on my back. They put me through a CAT scan followed by an MRI for my head injury. The doctor said I had swelling at the base of my parietal lobe, but no bleeding on the brain. Since I didn't have any major head injury symptoms, he kept me overnight for observation, and then let me go home.

And by home, I mean Parker's. Parker wouldn't let me out of his sight for two days. Not until day three, when I was able to finally shift. Buzz talked to the scientist who had told him about the fertility solution, about what happened, and the guy said he was going to study that area of a shifter's brain and see if it is tied to our abilities.

Frankly, I was just glad to feel my inner feline once more. I didn't know how much she was a part of me until she was gone.

Friday, the day before the open house, Bobby Morris allowed me to go visit Jordan Deeter in prison. She sat across from me, a glass divider between us. I picked up the receiver on my end and waited for her to do the same. She stared at me for a few minutes as if debating whether she would.

I breathed a sigh of relief when she finally grabbed it and put it to her ear.

"How are you?" I asked.

"My lawyer wants me to take an insanity plea." She shook her head. "I'm not crazy."

"You turned your house into a cooler to keep your dead mom fresh while you killed the men you blamed."

She mushed her lips together then half-smiled. "That sounds a little crazy," she finally said.

"It really does," I agreed. "Look, grief can make you nuts. Believe me. I've had my share of vengeful feelings. Take the deal."

Her shoulders slumped. "I would have done it," she said. "I would have killed Hanley if given a chance. The fact that I still want to do it—"

"Means you need a lot of help," I said.

Can you tell your cousin I'm sorry? I just panicked. I hadn't planned for Jock to figure out that I was poisoning him. He came at me, so I stabbed him. I knew he and Jock had fought because Jock had a black eye and raged about it when he came to the house."

"How did you get him out to your car to drive him?" Jordan wasn't much bigger than me, and Jock had outweighed her by a good fifty pounds.

"He was still on his feet. I told him I'd take him to the hospital. So, he got in on his own. He looked so close to death that I just pushed him out into the parking lot and drove off."

"And then used the app to spoof the sheriff's department."

"I don't feel good about it, believe me. It's the only part of this I regret. Well, that and hitting you, and well, not punishing Hanley."

"Speaking of Hanley. I thought you'd like to know that he's going to get what's coming to him. Anna Avery came forward about his gaming and racketeering, public fraud, and property schemes. She's turning into the state's best witness for a sweetheart deal to keep herself and her husband out of jail. If it makes you feel better, Hanley is going to get a life sentence. He'll have a lot of time to think about the lives he's ruined, including his own."

Jordan leaned forward. Her smile widened. She placed

her free hand against the glass. "Thank you, Lily," she said. "I do feel better."

SATURDAY MORNING ARRIVED, AND PARKER HAD BARELY slept the night before. He was so nervous about the open house. All the volunteers, whether it was their shifts or not, showed up. They helped us dress the dogs in cute accessories that made them look adorably adoptable. Smooshie wore a pink tutu, and I dressed Elvis with a tux dickie and a bowtie. Parker shook his head at me, but he didn't complain. Smooshie and Elvis were the perfect ambassadors for the breed, and we needed to use every tool in our arsenal.

It had been a good week. Buzz was free, my cougar was back, all the people who needed to be in jail were in jail, and our rescue dogs had a brand-new home where they could really be safe.

I watched as Keith made balloon animals for children, Larry was working a popcorn stand that the high school loaned us for the event, and Theresa was selling pit bull gear, T-shirts, hats, totes, and calendars. More than sixty people had shown up before noon, and we'd managed to get the paperwork rolling for a couple who wanted to adopt Star. She'd been without a forever home for so long, that I prayed they checked out, and Star would finally get all the love and attention she deserved.

Theresa had come back to work, but there was still

tension between us. She said she didn't blame me for her parents' legal trouble, but I didn't know how she couldn't. But she was cordial, and I would take it for now, because it was better than her hating me.

I slipped under Parker's arm and put mine around his waist. "Are you happy?" I asked.

He dipped his head and kissed me. "So much happy."

The End

MR. & MRS. SHIFT - CHAPTER 1

WITCHIN' IMPOSSIBLE COZY MYSTERIES
BOOK 4

A witchy bride. An itchy groom. A flower girl squirrel.
And a dead wedding planner. Why is nothing ever easy
in Paradise Falls.

Witch Hazel Kinsey is finally marrying the love of her life, werebear Ford Baylor, in a ceremony that will bind their souls for life.

Unfortunately, party crashers have other plans for the anxious bride. Like killing her before the ceremony. Haze and Ford, with the help of Tizzy the squirrel, and Lily Mason are determined to track down the killer and make the midnight deadline, but if they can't stop the person behind the bounty on Haze's head, the wedding may be off. Permanently.

What's a Witchzilla to do when everything on her special day goes wrong? Everything she can to make sure she doesn't lose her one shot at true happiness.

For Hazel and the gang, it's just another day in Paradise Falls.

Available at All Your Favorite eTailers

Chapter One

"Well, that's it. The wedding is off," chirped Tizzy, my familiar, a red flying squirrel with a flair for the dramatic. Although, in this case, there was a reason for the drama.

"The wedding is not off," I whispered harshly.

"Hazel, you no longer have a wedding planner!"

"I don't need a wedding planner," I countered. "Especially one who just tried to kill me, for goddess' sake. Now, help me hide the body."

I manufactured a calm demeanor. Which was difficult. My wedding planner, Vivi Lashay, a perky and enthusiastic witch, who had been my confidant and closest ally in my war on flowers and cake, had just tried to shoot me with a silenced Walther PK380. That was the weapon of an assassin, not a person who specialized in making brides feel special.

"Goddess, Haze," said my BFF-since-kindergarten Lily Mason. She leaned over, holding her long, auburn hair back with one hand so the silky strands wouldn't fall into the corpse. "Smells remarkably like barbeque mixed with ozone."

"Ewww." Tizzy skittered up to my shoulder. "You cooked her."

I gagged but managed to get it under control before dry heaves started. I had a very active gag reflex, a fact that could make some things in the bedroom more difficult, but I'd learned how to control it somewhat during my fifteen years at the FBI working serial killings and murders—and let's not forget Peter the Prick, the only flasher to ever make the FBI's most-wanted list. Trust me. He deserved prison time for waggling that diseased-pocked penis at unsuspecting women. However, Lily was right. Vivi smelled decidedly charbroiled.

Well, that was that. I'd never eat barbecue again.

Gak! I put my fingers against my lips.

"Are you going to puke?" asked Tizzy.

"No. And don't say puke." I swallowed my gorge. "Okay. The sendoff party is in a couple of hours." I tugged the hem of my slip over my knees, side-stepped Vivi's body, and used my toe to nudge the gun out of her lifeless hand.

Lily shook her head. "I heard the last time someone did the bonding ceremony out here, the bride got hit by lightning. It might just be the place. Bad luck and all."

Bindings were a rarity, and I hadn't heard of any ceremonies taking place since I took over as Chief of Police. "When did this happen?"

"A long time ago. Like when we were kids. It wasn't anyone my parents knew, so I could be remembering wrong. Still. Maybe we should cancel the binding or at least postpone it."

"No!" I said emphatically. "I am not canceling. I am not canceling anything." In Paradise Falls, the town is half witches, half shifters. Shifters mated for life, while witches were more like humans, in that marriages didn't always last. The founders, in their wisdom, put a halt to fly-by-night nuptials by creating a bonding spell that prevented witches from breaking their vows. The ceremony would take place at midnight tonight under the Goddess's Light Temple aka an open gazebo on the lake.

The sendoff would end at ten o'clock, and I would return to the room to change into my wedding gown and receive blessings from all the female guests before they followed me out to the gazebo to meet Ford and take his soul to mine.

Then we would be genuinely mated and wed by both witch and shifter standards. Breaking the bonds required some dark and deadly magic. I knew that for a fact. After all, my father had obliterated my mom when he'd separated his life force from hers.

Don't worry. She had it coming.

Even so, Dad had spent seventeen years in witch jail for the crime. Since Dad and Mom's break-up via explosive magic, the bonding ceremony had become optional. But since Ford didn't have a choice in loving me for the rest of his life, I wasn't going to be any less committed. I would happily join my soul to his over and over again, but that meant we needed witnesses. The binding fed off physical energy, so the more witnesses, the stronger the binding, and I'd opened the invitation to my witchy wedded bliss to everyone I could think of. I wasn't sure if I could get this many people to show up twice.

"No," I said again. "No postponement. We have twenty-eight RSVPs arriving for dinner and close to two hundred more for the sendoff party, including some family from out of town, and I'm not going to turn them all away because of one itty bitty well-deserved death." I'm pretty sure I sounded hysterical, but I didn't care. I'd been planning for this week since November, and I could see my whole wedding going the way of Vivi Lashay.

Tiz, from my shoulder, looked down at the cooked wedding planner and whistled. "Goddess in a tutu, Haze. You burned a hole clean through her."

A tunnel the width of a softball had replaced the area where Vivi's heart used to be located. It had created a passage, cauterizing her flesh, arteries, and veins as it traveled through her body. I frowned. "I didn't mean to." My witch powers had been getting stronger over the past year and a half, ever since I'd come back home, but my ability to control them hadn't progressed as fast. The results were sometimes disastrous. "I only meant to shock her."

"That's not shocked." Tizzy pressed her tiny fingers to her chest. "I'm shocked." She pointed at the corpse. "That's a full-scale electrocution. The only thing missing is the electric chair."

"If she hadn't tried to shoot me, I wouldn't have had to defend myself." I walked to the window and stared out at the wedding guests milling around the yard. I was feeling shaky from the near-death experience. "Barbecued assassin is the last thing I need right now."

Lily joined me and put her arm around my shoulders. "Nobody needs this kind of thing, honey. Especially when you're trying to marry your soulmate. Even so, I'm wondering if maybe I shouldn't have your father translocate Parker back to Moonrise and wipe his memory of Paradise Falls."

I watched Lily's human boyfriend, Parker Knowles, having a conversation with my soon to be father-in-law. Parker laughed at something Brent Baylor said, and Brent smiled, which, in turn, made me smile. Parker knew that Lily was a cougar shifter for almost a year now, and it hadn't mattered. Lily waved to Parker from the window. He smiled up at her and waved back. He loved her. Even a blind witch could see just how much.

I patted my best friend's hand. "We are back on the Happiness Train as of now, so Parker stays. You two are adorable together, and he seems to be handling the whole supernatural town thing pretty well."

"On account, he hasn't seen the dead girl," she said. She sighed wistfully. "What if I can't protect him? You know, if the florist tries to stab you or something, and you go nuclear."

"It'll be fine." I hoped. I wish I knew why Vivian had tried to shoot me. The short time I'd been back home, I had made a few enemies. The witches who had supported Adele Adams, and the families of Jenny Weaver and Romy Quinn. Plus, I was pretty sure the High Clowder would love to see me taken down a peg or two. Even so, I didn't think any of them would hire an assassin to take me out. I know it was selfish, but I couldn't help but wish Vivi had at least waited until the reception to take me out. Now, I had to do all the wedding coordination without any professional help.

A sharp knock at the door made me yelp.

"Everything okay in there?" My father, Kent Kinsey, was doing the traditional dad thing and giving me away. This antiquated ritual based on the idea that I was somehow property to be given away made my dad happy. I liked seeing him happy. Even if it sometimes grossed me out. For example, he and his plus one—*yuck*—were staying in the Celestial Suite, across from the Groom's Room and next to the Bride's. Which meant, we shared a wall. I had warned him that I better not hear any monkey-rooster noises coming from that direction or else. Or else what? I had no idea, but I'd make sure it wasn't pretty. What I didn't take into consideration was that he could hear noises coming from my room as well. I had apologized more than once at breakfast for scarring him for life.

"It's fine," I lied. "Everything is A-okay."

Lily said in a hushed voice, "Maybe we should just tell him. He might be able to help."

I shook my head.

"I heard shouting," Dad said.

I looked at Lily for help with a good lie. She shrugged. Absolutely no help at all. I rolled my eyes at her. She stuck out her tongue.

"Real mature," I whispered.

She grinned.

With no input from the peanut gallery, I turned to the

door and said to my dad, "It's a new stress release technique called Scream Your Pain."

"Are you sure it's not called Getting Cold Feet?" he asked.

"No!" As if. There was nothing cold about my feet or my feelings for Ford Baylor.

"Can I come in?"

"No!" shouted Tizzy, Lily, and I at the same time.

My father had a penchant for translocating into a room on a dime, so I added, "I'm naked."

"All right. I'll check on you in a bit."

"Thanks, Dad." I gave Tizzy side-eye. "Find me a place to put Vivi until I can think of something better. People are going to be traipsing in and out of this room for an hour before the ceremony, and I can't have them tripping over her corpse."

"Why don't you just use your magic and store her somewhere private, I don't know, like say, Wyoming, until after the festivities," Lily said.

"My magic is unpredictable when I'm feeling calm. When I'm not calm," I gestured to the body, "I blow holes in people. Knowing my luck, I'd shoot for Wyoming and end up with an inside out Vivi on my cake table."

"Fair point," Lily said. "Nothing ruins a good wedding ceremony like corpse cake-topper."

Tizzy sighed. "You know, hiding a body is very un-cop-like behavior?" She affected disappointment. "You're the chief of police. This could seriously affect your re-election."

I shooed her off my shoulder. "It won't matter if someone murders me."

Tizzy jumped onto the vanity. "Now who's being dramatic."

"You weren't here when she pointed that gun at me. Trust me, no extra drama here." I glanced at Lily. "I think you better find Ford."

Tizzy sighed theatrically. "Do we really have to involve old furry, saggy butt?"

"He has a middle-aged, sexy, firm as hell butt, and no fur on it, at least not when he's in his human form."

"Is this really the best topic of conversation considering the—" Tizzy gestured to the body.

"You think she cares?" I looked at Lily. "Will you get Ford for me?"

"Of course," she said.

The high-pitched voice of doom said, "Isn't it bad luck to see the bride before the wedding?"

"Don't be daft. Besides, I don't think my luck can get any worse."

Lily flinched. "Did you really have to say that? It's like

inviting the Bad Luck demons to up the ante."

"Death by electric zap is gonna be hard to top." Tizzy jumped off my shoulder, spread her arms and legs, and glided to the vanity. Her soft, proficient landing would have given Superman a run for his money. She gave me a final look of disdain. "All I have to do is find a hiding spot for a dead wedding planner in a farmhouse full of people. Nooo problem."

Lily squeezed my hand. She walked to the door and opened it a crack. "I'll be right back with Ford."

"Don't you mean Fuzzy Wuzzy," Tiz corrected and slid through the opening.

"Please don't call--" Tizzy was gone before I could finish.

Lily looked sympathetic. "I can talk to her if you want. I think she's just scared."

"Of what? I think I've proven I'll go to great lengths to not lose her." I'd even given up being a witch, which royally blew, for a short period of time when the High Clowder, which is just a formal way of saying a familiar council made up of a bunch of stuck-up cats, had tried to take her away from me and assign me some hairless nimrod named Lonnie in her stead. When I refused, they stripped me of my magic.

Let me just say here and now, being human, even for a couple of days, sucked ginormous, non-magical, hairy balls.

"I was willing to give up everything that makes me who I am to save Tiz."

"She knows that on an intellectual level, but emotionally... She's always been the most important being in your life until you moved back to Paradise Falls. Even though you and Ford are already mates, making it official with this binding will make it official with Tizzy that she has to share you for the rest of your long, long life."

I hoped it was a long life. I almost died fifteen minutes ago, and the day wasn't over yet. "She's got a girlfriend, Lils."

"Who you dislike for the same reasons she doesn't always like Ford."

"In my defense, the cat hated me long before I hated her." But I had to admit that occasionally it hurt when Tiz would blow me off to spend time with Loopydoopy.

Lily laughed. Surprising, considering our current circumstance. "True story."

I huffed. "I'll talk to her."

"I'll be right back with your beau."

After Lily left, I got up and shuffled to the window. I sniffled. As tears streamed my cheeks, the mineral mask on my face loosened and made the clay all gloopy. Damn it. This couldn't be happening. Not on my wedding eve.

Want to read more? Get it today!

www.witchinimpossible.com

PARANORMAL MYSTERIES & ROMANCES

BY RENEE GEORGE

Witchin' Impossible Cozy Mysteries

www.witchinimpossible.com

Witchin' Impossible (Book 1)

Rogue Coven (Book 2)

Familiar Protocol (Booke 3)

Mr & Mrs. Shift (Book 4)

Barkside of the Moon Mysteries

www.barksideofthemoonmysteries.com

Pit Perfect Murder (Book 1)

Murder & The Money Pit (Book 2)

The Pit List Murders (Book 3)

Peculiar Mysteries

www.peculiarmysteries.com

You've Got Tail (Book 1) FREE Download

My Furry Valentine (Book 2)

Thank You For Not Shifting (Book 3)

My Hairy Halloween (Book 4)

In the Midnight Howl (Book 5)

My Peculiar Road Trip (Magic & Mayhem) (Book 6)

Furred Lines (Book7)

My Wolfy Wedding (Book 8)

Who Let The Wolves Out? (Book 9)

Madder Than Hell

www.madder-than-hell.com

Gone With The Minion (Book 1)

Devil On A Hot Tin Roof (Book 2)

A Street Car Named Demonic (Book 3)

Hex Drive

https://www.renee-george.com/hex-drive-series

Hex Me, Baby, One More Time (Book 1)

ABOUT THE AUTHOR

I am a USA Today Bestselling author who writes paranormal mysteries and romances because I love all things whodunit, Otherworldly, and weird. Also, I wish my pittie, the adorable Kona Princess Warrior, and my beagle, Josie the Incontinent Princess, could talk. Or at least be more like Scooby-Doo and help me unmask villains at the haunted house up the street.

When I'm not writing about mystery-solving werecougars or the adventures of a hapless psychic living among shapeshifters, I am preyed upon by stray kittens who end up living in my house because I can't say no to those sweet, furry faces. (Someone stop telling them where I live!)

I live in Mid-Missouri with my family and I spend my non-writing time doing really cool stuff...like watching TV and cleaning up dog poop.

Follow Me On Bookbub!